Deadwood Dick:
The Prince of the Road

Edward L. Wheeler

Copyrighted in 1877, by BEADLE AND ADAMS.

Vol. I. Single Number. BEADLE AND ADAMS, PUBLISHERS, No. 98 WILLIAM STREET, NEW YORK. Price, 5 Cents. No. 1

Deadwood Dick

THE PRINCE OF THE ROAD;

OR,

THE BLACK RIDER OF THE BLACK HILLS.

BY EDWARD L. WHEELER.

CHAPTER I.

FEARLESS FRANK TO THE RESCUE.

On the plains, midway between Cheyenne and the Black Hills, a train had halted for a noonday feed. Not a railway train, mind you, but a line of those white-covered vehicles drawn by strong-limbed mules, which are most properly styled "prairie schooners."

There were four wagons of this type, and they had been drawn in a circle about a camp-fire, over which was roasting a savory haunch of venison. Around the camp-fire were grouped half a score of men, all rough, bearded, and grizzled, with one exception. This being a youth whose age one could have safely put at twenty, so perfectly developed of physique and intelligent of facial appearance was he. There was something about him that was not handsome, and yet you would have been puzzled to tell what it was, for his countenance was strikingly handsome, and surely no form in the crowd was more noticeable for its grace, symmetry, and proportionate development. It would have taken a scholar to have studied out the secret.

He was of about medium stature, and as straight and square-shouldered as an athlete. His complexion was nut-brown, from long exposure to the sun; hair of hue of the raven's wing, and hanging in long, straight strands adown his back; eyes black and piercing as an eagle's; features well molded, with a firm, resolute mouth and prominent chin. He was an interesting specimen of young, healthy manhood, and, even though a youth in years, was one that could command respect, if not admiration, wheresoever he might choose to go.

One remarkable item about his personal appearance, apt to strike the beholder as being exceedingly strange and eccentric, was his costume—buck-skin throughout, and that dyed to the brightest scarlet hue.

On being asked the cause of his odd freak of dress, when he had joined the train a few miles out from Cheyenne, the youth had laughingly replied:

1

"Why, you see, it is to attract bufflers, if we should meet any, out on the plains 'twixt this and the Hills."

He gave his name as Fearless Frank, and said he was aiming for the Hills; that if the party in question would furnish him a place among them, he would extend to them his assistance as a hunter, guide, or whatever, until the destination was reached.

Seeing that he was well armed, and judging from external appearances that he would prove a valuable accessory, the miners were nothing loth in accepting his services.

Of the others grouped about the camp-fire only one is specially noticeable, for, as Mark Twain remarks, "the average of gold-diggers look alike." This person was a little, deformed old man; hump-backed, bow-legged, and white-haired, with cross eyes, a large mouth, a big head, set upon a slim, crane-like neck; blue eyes, and an immense brown beard, that flowed downward half-way to the belt about his waist, which contained a small arsenal of knives and revolvers. He hobbled about with a heavy crutch constantly under his left arm, and was certainly a pitiable sight to behold.

He too had joined the caravan after it had quitted Cheyenne, his advent taking place about an hour subsequent to that of Fearless Frank. His name he asserted was Nix—Geoffrey Walsingham Nix— and where he came from, and what he sought in the Black Hills, was simply a matter of conjecture among the miners, as he refused to talk on the subject of his past, present or future.

The train was under the command of an irascible old plainsman who had served out his apprenticeship in the Kansas border war, and whose name was Charity Joe, which, considering his avaricious disposition, was the wrong handle on the wrong man. Charity was the least of all old Joe's redeeming characteristics; charity was the very thing he did not recognize, yet some wag had facetiously branded him Charity Joe, and the appellation had clung to him ever since. He was well advanced in years, yet withal a good trailer and an expert guide, as the success of his many late expeditions into the Black Hills had evidenced.

Those who had heard of Joe's skill as a guide, intrusted themselves in his care, for, while the stages were stopped more or less on each trip, Charity Joe's train invariably went through all safe and sound. This was partly owing to his acquaintance with various bands of Indians, who were the chief cause of annoyance on the trip.

So far we see the train toward the land of gold, without their having seen sight or sound of hostile red-skins, and Charity is just chuckling over his usual good luck:

"I tell ye what, fellers, we've hed a fa'r sort uv a shake, so fur, an' no mistake 'bout it. Barrin' thar ain't no Sittin' Bulls layin' in wait fer us, behead yander, in ther mounts, I'm of ther candid opinion we'll get through wi'out scrapin' a ha'r."

"I hope so," said Fearless Frank, rolling over on the grass and gazing at the guide, thoughtfully, "but I doubt it. It seems to me that one hears of more butchering, lately, than there was a month ago—all on account of the influx of ruffianly characters into the Black Hills!"

"Not all owing to that, chippy," interposed "General" Nix, as he had immediately been christened by the miners—"not all owing to that. Thar's them gol danged copper-colored guests uv ther government—they're kickin' up three pints uv the'r rumpus, more or less—consider'bly less of more than more o' less. Take a passel uv them barbarities an' shet 'em up inter a prison for three or thirteen yeers, an' ye'd see w'at an impression et'd make, now. Thar'd be siveral less massycrees a week, an' ye wouldn't see a rufyan onc't a month. W'y, gentlefellows, thar'd nevyar been a ruffian, ef et hedn't been fer ther cussed Injun tribe—not *one!* Ther infarnal critters ar' ther instignators uv more deviltry nor a cat wi' nine tails."

"Yes, we will admit that the reds are not of saintly origin," said Fearless Frank, with a quiet smile. "In fact I know of several who are far from being angels, myself. There is old Sitting Bull, for instance, and Lone Lion, Rain-in-the-Face, and Horse-with-the-Red-Eye, and so forth, and so forth!"

"Exactly. Every one o' 'em's a danged descendant o' ther old Satan, hisself."

"Layin' aside ther Injun subjeck," said Charity Joe, forking into the roasted venison, "I move thet we take up a silent debate on ther pecooliarities uv a deer's hind legs; so heer goes!"

3

He cut out a huge slice with his bowie, sprinkled it over with salt, and began to devour it by very large mouthfuls. All hands proceeded to follow his example, and the noonday meal was dispatched in silence. After each man had fully satisfied his appetite and the mules and Fearless Frank's horse had grazed until they were full as ticks, the order was given to hitch up, which was speedily done, and the caravan was soon in motion, toiling along like a diminutive serpent across the plain.

The afternoon was a mild, sunny one in early autumn, with a refreshing breeze perfumed with the delicate scent of after-harvest flowers wafting down from the cool regions of the Northwest, where lay the new El Dorado—the land of gold.

Fearless Frank bestrode a noble bay steed of fire and nerve, while old General Nix rode an extra mule that he had purchased of Charity Joe. The remainder of the company rode in the wagons or "hoofed it," as best suited their mood—walking sometimes being preferable to the rumbling and jolting of the heavy vehicles.

Steadily along through the afternoon sunlight the train wended its way, the teamsters alternately singing and cursing their mules, as they jogged along. Fearless Frank and the "General" rode several hundred yards in advance, both apparently engrossed in deepest thought, for neither spoke until, toward the close of the afternoon, Charity Joe called their attention to a series of low, faint cries brought down upon their hearing by the stiff northerly wind.

"'Pears to me as how them sound sorter human like," said the old guide, trotting along beside the young man's horse, as he made known the discovery. "Jes' listen, now, an' see if ye ain't uv ther same opinion!"

The youth did listen, and at the same time swept the plain with his eagle eyes, in search of the object from which the cries emanated. But nothing of animal life was visible in any direction beyond the train, and more was the mystery, since the cries sounded but a little way off.

"They *are* human cries!" exclaimed Fearless Frank, excitedly, "and come from some one in distress. Boys, we must investigate this matter."

"You can investigate all ye want," grunted Charity Joe, "but I hain't a-goin' ter stop ther train till dusk, squawk or no squawk. I jedge we won't get inter their Hills any too soon, as it ar'."

"You're an old fool!" retorted Frank, contemptuously. "I wouldn't be as mean as you for all the gold in the Black Hills country, say nothin' about that in California and Colorado."

He turned his horse's head toward the north, and rode away, followed, to the wonder of all, by the "General."

"Ha! ha!" laughed Charity Joe, grimly, "I wish you success."

"You needn't; I do not want any of your wishes. I'm going to search for the person who makes them cries, an' ef you don't want to wait, why go to the deuce with your old train!"

"There ye err," shouted the guide: "I'm goin' ter Deadwood, instead uv ter the deuce."

"*Maybe* you will go to Deadwood, and then, again, maybe ye won't," answered back Fearless Frank.

"More or less!" chimed in the general—"consider'bly more of less than less of more. Look out thet ther allies uv Sittin' Bull don't git ther *dead wood* on ye."

On marched the train—steadily on over the level, sandy plain, and Fearless Frank and his strange companion turned their attention to the cries that had been the means of separating them from the train. They had ceased now, altogether, and the two men were at a loss what to do.

"Guv a whoop, like a Government Injun," suggested "General" Nix; "an' thet'll let ther critter know thet we be friends a-comin'. Par'ps she'm g'in out ontirely, a-thinkin' as no one war a-comin' ter her resky!"

"She, you say?"

"Yas, she; fer I calkylate 'twern't no *he* as made them squawks. Sing out like a bellerin' bull, now, an' et ar' more or less likely— consider'bly more of less 'n less of more—that she will respond!"

Fearless Frank laughed, and forming his hands into a trumpet he gave vent to a loud, ear-splitting "hello!" that made the prairies ring.

"Great whale uv Joner!" gasped the "General," holding his hands toward the region of his organs of hearing. "Holy Mother o' Mercy! don't do et ag'in, b'yee—don' do et; ye've smashed my tinpanum all inter flinders! Good heaven! ye hev got a bugle wus nor enny steam tooter frum heer tew Lowell."

"Hark!" said the youth, bending forward in a listening attitude.

The next instant silence prevailed, and the twain anxiously listened. Wafted down across the plain came in faint piteous accents the repetition of the cry they had first heard, only it was now much fainter. Evidently whoever was in distress, was weakening rapidly. Soon the cries would be inaudible.

"It's straight ahead!" exclaimed Fearless Frank, at last. "Come along, and we'll soon see what the matter is!"

He put the spurs to his spirited animal, and the next instant was dashing wildly off over the sunlit plain. Bent on emulation, the "General" also used his heels with considerable vim, but alas! what dependence can be placed on a mule? The animal bolted, with a vicious nip back at the offending rider's legs, and refused to budge an inch.

On—on dashed the fearless youth, mounted on his noble steed, his eyes bent forward, in a sharp scrutiny of the plain ahead, his mind filled with wonder that the cries were now growing more distinct and yet not a first glimpse could he obtain of the source whence they emanated.

On—on—on; then suddenly he reins his steed back upon its haunches, just in time to avert a frightful plunge into one of those remarkable freaks of nature—the blind canal, or, in other words, a channel valley washed out by heavy rains. These the tourist will frequently encounter in the regions contiguous to the Black Hills.

Below him yawned an abrupt channel, a score or more of feet in depth, at the bottom of which was a dense chaparral thicket. The little valley thus nestled in the earth was about forty rods in width, and one would never have dreamed it existed, unless they chanced to ride to the brink, above.

Fearless Frank took in the situation at a glance, and not hearing the cries, he rightly conjectured that the one in distress had again become exhausted. That that person was in the thicket below seemed more than probable, and he immediately resolved to descend in search. Slipping from his saddle, he stepped forward to the very edge of the precipice and looked over. The next second the ground crumbled beneath his feet, and he was precipitated headlong into the valley. Fortunately he received no serious injuries, and in a moment was on his feet again, all right.

"A miss is as good as a mile," he muttered, brushing the dirt from his clothing. "Now, then, we will find out the secret of the racket in this thicket."

Glancing up to the brink above to see that his horse was standing quietly, he parted the shrubbery, and entered the thicket.

It required considerable pushing and tugging to get through the dense undergrowth, but at last his efforts were rewarded, and he stood in a small break or glade.

Stood there, to behold a sight that made the blood boil in his veins. Securely bound with her face toward a stake, was a young girl—a maiden of perhaps seventeen summers, whom, at a single glance, one might surmise was remarkably pretty.

She was stripped to the waist, and upon her snow-white back were numerous welts from which trickled diminutive rivulets of crimson. Her head was dropped against the stake to which she was bound, and she was evidently insensible.

With a cry of astonishment and indignation Fearless Frank leaped forward to sever her bonds, when like so many grim phantoms there filed out of the chaparral, and circled around him, a score of hideously painted savages. One glance at the portly leader satisfied Frank as to his identity. It was the fiend incarnate—Sitting Bull!

CHAPTER II.

DEADWOOD DICK, THE ROAD-AGENT.

"$500 Reward: For the apprehension and arrest of a notorious young desperado who hails to the name of Deadwood Dick. His present whereabouts are somewhat contiguous to the Black Hills. For further information, and so forth, apply immediately to

HUGH VANSEVERE,

"At Metropolitan Saloon, Deadwood City."

Thus read a notice posted up against a big pine tree, three miles above Custer City, on the banks of French creek. It was a large placard tacked up in plain view of all passers-by who took the route north through Custer gulch in order to reach the infant city of the Northwest—Deadwood.

Deadwood! the scene of the most astonishing bustle and activity, this year (1877.) The place where men are literally made rich and poor in one day and night. Prior to 1877 the Black Hills have been for a greater part undeveloped, but now, what a change! In Deadwood districts every foot of available ground has been "claimed" and staked out; the population has increased from fifteen to more than twenty-five hundred souls.

The streets are swarming with constantly arriving new-comers; the stores and saloons are literally crammed at all hours; dance-houses and can-can dens exist; hundreds of eager, expectant, and hopeful miners are working in the mines, and the harvest reaped by them is not at all discouraging. All along the gulch are strung a profusion of cabins, tents and shanties, making Deadwood in reality a town of a dozen miles in length, though some enterprising individual has paired off a couple more infant cities above Deadwood proper, named respectively Elizabeth City and Ten Strike. The quartz formation in these neighborhoods is something extraordinary, and

8

from late reports, under vigorous and earnest development are yielding beyond the most sanguine expectation.

The placer mines west of Camp Crook are being opened to very satisfactory results, and, in fact, from Custer City in the south, to Deadwood in the north, all is the scene of abundant enthusiasm and excitement.

A horseman riding north through Custer gulch, noticed the placard so prominently posted for public inspection, and with a low whistle, expressive of astonishment, wheeled his horse out of the stage road, and rode over to the foot of the tree in question, and ran his eyes over the few irregularly-written lines traced upon the notice.

He was a youth of an age somewhere between sixteen and twenty, trim and compactly built, with a preponderance of muscular development and animal spirits; broad and deep of chest, with square, iron-cast shoulders; limbs small yet like bars of steel, and with a grace of position in the saddle rarely equaled; he made a fine picture for an artist's brush or a poet's pen.

Only one thing marred the captivating beauty of the picture.

His form was clothed in a tight-fitting habit of buck-skin, which was colored a jetty black, and presented a striking contrast to anything one sees as a garment in the wild far West. And this was not all, either. A broad black hat was slouched down over his eyes; he wore a thick black vail over the upper portion of his face, through the eye-holes of which there gleamed a pair of orbs of piercing intensity, and his hands, large and knotted, were hidden in a pair of kid gloves of a light color.

The "Black Rider" he might have been justly termed, for his thoroughbred steed was as black as coal, but we have not seen fit to call him such—his name is Deadwood Dick, and let that suffice for the present.

It was just at the edge of evening that he stopped before, and proceeded to read, the placard posted upon the tree in one of the loneliest portions of Custer's gulch.

Above and on either side rose to a stupendous hight the tree-fringed mountains in all their majestic grandeur.

In front and behind, running nearly north and south, lay the deep, dark chasm—a rift between mighty walls—Custer's gulch.

And over all began to hover the cloak of night, for the sun had already imparted its dying kiss on the mountain craters, and below, the gloom was thickening with rapid strides.

Slowly, over and over, Deadwood Dick, outlaw, road-agent and outcast, read the notice, and then a wild sardonic laugh burst from beneath his mask—a terrible, blood-curdling laugh, that made even the powerful animal he bestrode start and prick up its ears.

"Five hundred dollars reward for the apprehension and arrest of a notorious young desperado who hails to the name of Deadwood Dick! Ha! ha! ha! isn't that rich, now? Ha! ha! ha! *arrest* Deadwood Dick! Why, 'pon my word it is a sight for sore eyes. I was not aware that I had attained such a desperate notoriety as that document implies. They will make me out a murderer before they get through, I expect. Can't let me alone—everlastingly they must be punching after me, as if I was some obnoxious pestilence on the face of the earth. Never mind, though—let 'em keep on! Let them just continue their hounding game, and see which comes up on top when the bag's shook. If more than one of 'em don't get their fingers burned when they snatch Deadwood Dick bald-headed, why I'm a Spring creek sucker, that's all. Maybe I don't know who foots the bill in this reward business; oh, no; maybe I can't ride down to Deadwood and frighten three kind o' ideas out of this Mr. Hugh Vansevere, whoever he may be. Ha! ha! the fool that h'isted that notice didn't *know* Deadwood Dick, or he would never have placed his life in jeopardy by performing an act so uninteresting to the party in question. Hugh Vansevere; let me see—I don't think I've got that registered in my collection of appellatives. Perhaps he is a new tool in the employ of the old mechanic."

Darker and thicker grew the night shadows. The after-harvest moon rose up to a sufficient hight to send a silvery bolt of powerful light down into the silent gulch; like an image carved out of the night the horse and rider stood before the placard, motionless, silent.

The head of Deadwood Dick was bent, and he was buried in a deep reverie. A reverie that engrossed his whole attention for a long, long while; then the impatient pawing of his horse aroused him, and he sat once more erect in his saddle.

A last time his eyes wandered over the notice on the tree—a last time his terrible laugh made the mountains ring, and he guided his horse back into the rough, uneven stage-road, and galloped off up the gulch.

"I will go and see what this Hugh Vansevere looks like!" he said, applying the spurs to his horse. "I'll be dashed if I want him to be so numerous with my name, especially with five hundred dollars affixed thereto, as a reward."

Ha! ha! ha! isn't that rich, now? Ha! ha! ha! arrest Deadwood Dick if you can!

Midnight.

Camp Crook, nestling down in one of the wildest gulch pockets of the Black Hills region—basking and sleeping in the flood of moonlight that emanates from the glowing ball up afar in heaven's blue vault, is suddenly and rudely aroused from her dreams.

There is a wild clatter of hoofs, a chorus of strange and varied voices swelling out in a wild mountain song, and up through the very heart of the diminutive city, where the gold-fever has dropped a few sanguine souls, dash a cavalcade of masked horsemen, attired in the picturesque garb of the mountaineer, and mounted on animals of superior speed and endurance.

At their head, looking weird and wonderful in his suit of black, rides he whom all have heard of—he whom some have seen, and he whom no one dare raise a hand against, in single combat—Deadwood Dick, Road-Agent Prince, and the one person whose name is in everybody's mouth.

Straight on through the single northerly street of the infant village ride the dauntless band, making weirdly beautiful music with their rollicking song, some of the voices being cultivated, and clear as the clarion note.

A few miners, wakened from their repose, jump out of bed, come to the door, and stare at the receding cavalcade in a dazed sort of way. Others, thinking that the noise is all resulting from an Indian attack, seize rifles or revolvers, as the case may be, and blaze away out of windows and loopholes at whatever may be in the way to receive their bullets.

But the road-agents only pause a moment in their song to send back a wild, sarcastic laugh; then they resume it, and merrily dash along up the gulch, the ringing of iron-shod hoofs beating a strange tatoo to the sound of the music.

Sleepily the miners crawl back to their respective couches; the moon smiles down on mother earth, and nature once more fans itself to sleep with the breath of a fragrant breeze.

Deadwood Dick: The Prince of the Road

Deadwood—magic city of the West!

Not dead, nor even sleeping, is this headquarters of the Black Hills population at midnight, twenty-four hours subsequent to the rush of the daring road-agents through Camp Crook.

Deadwood is just as lively and hilarious a place during the interval between sunset and sunrise as during the day. Saloons, dance-houses, and gambling dens keep open all night, and stores do not close until a late hour. At one, two and three o'clock in the morning the streets present as lively an appearance as at any period earlier in the evening. Fighting, shooting, stabbing and hideous swearing are features of the night; singing, drinking, dancing and gambling another.

Nightly the majority of the miners come in from such claims as are within a radius of from six to ten miles, and seldom is it that they go away without their "load." To be sure, there are some men in Deadwood who do not drink, but they are so few and scattering as to seem almost entirely a nonentity.

It was midnight, and Deadwood lay basking in a flood of mellow moonlight that cast long shadows from the pine forest on the peaks, and glinted upon the rapid, muddy waters of Whitewood creek, which rumbles noisily by the infant metropolis on its wild journey toward the south.

All the saloons and dance-houses are in full blast; shouts and maudlin yells rend the air. In front of one insignificant board, "ten-by-twenty," an old wretch is singing out lustily:

"Right this way ye cum, pilgrims, ter ther great Black Hills Thee'ter; only costs ye four bits ter go in an' see ther tender sex, already a-kickin' in their striped stockin's; only four bits, recollect, ter see ther greatest show on earth, so heer's yer straight chance!"

But, why the use of yelling? Already the shanty is packed, and judging from the thundering screeches and clapping of hands, the entertainment is such as suits the depraved tastes of the ruffianly "bums" who have paid their "four bits," and gone in.

But look!

Madly out of Deadwood gulch, the abode of thousands of lurking shadows, dashes a horseman.

Straight through the main street of the noisy metropolis he spurs, with hat off, and hair blowing backward in a jetty cloud.

On, on, followed by the eyes of scores curious to know the meaning of his haste—on, and at last he halts in front of a large board shanty, over whose doorway is the illuminated canvas sign: "Metropolitan Saloon, by Tom Young."

Evidently his approach is heard, for instantly out of the "Metropolitan" there swarms a crowd of miners, gamblers and bummers to see "what the row is."

"Is there a man among you, gentlemen, who bears the name of Hugh Vansevere?" asks the rider, who from his midnight dress we may judge is no other than Deadwood Dick.

"That is my handle, pilgrim!" and a tall, rough-looking customer of the Minnesotian order steps forward. "What mought yer lay be ag'in me?"

"A *sure* lay!" hisses the masked road-agent, sternly. "You are advertising for one Deadwood Dick, and he has come to pay you his respects!"

The next instant there is a flash, a pistol report, a fall and a groan, the clattering of iron-shod hoofs; and then, ere anyone scarcely dreams of it, *Deadwood Dick is gone!*

CHAPTER III.

THE "CATTYMOUNT"—A QUARREL AND ITS RESULTS.

The "Metropolitan" saloon in Deadwood, one week subsequent to the events last narrated, was the scene of a larger "jamboree" than for many weeks before.

It was Saturday night, and up from the mines of Gold Run, Bobtail, Poor Man's Pocket, and Spearfish, and down from the Deadwood in miniature, Crook City, poured a swarm of rugged, grisly gold-diggers, the blear-eyed, used-up-looking "pilgrim," and the inevitable wary sharp, ever on the alert for a new buck to fleece.

The "Metropolitan" was then, as now, the headquarters of the Black Hills metropolis for arriving trains and stages, and as a natural consequence received a goodly share of the public patronage.

A well-stocked bar of liquors in Deadwood was *non est* yet the saloon in question boasted the best to be had. Every bar has its clerk at a pair of tiny scales, and he is ever kept more than busy weighing out the shining dust that the toiling miner has obtained by the sweat of his brow. And if the deft-fingered clerk cannot put six ounces of dust in his own pouch of a night, it clearly shows that he is not long in the business.

Saturday night!

The saloon is full to overflowing—full of brawny rough, and grisly men; full of ribald songs and maudlin curses; full of foul atmospheres, impregnated with the fumes of vile whisky, and worse tobacco, and full of sights and scenes, exciting and repulsive.

As we enter and work our way toward the center of the apartment, our attention is attracted by a coarse, brutal "tough," evidently just fresh in from the diggings; who, mounted on the summit of an empty whisky cask, is exhorting in rough language, and in the tones of a bellowing bull, to an audience of admiring miners assembled at his feet, which, by the way, are not of the most diminutive pattern imaginable. We will listen:

"Feller coots and liquidarians, behold before ye a real descendant uv Cain and Abel. Ye'll reckolect, ef ye've ever bin ter camp-meetin', that Abel got knocked out o' time by his cuzzin Cain, an becawse Abel war misproperly named, and warn't *able* when the crysis arriv ter defen' himsel' in an able manner.

"Hed he bin 'heeled' wi' a shipment uv Black Hills sixes, thet would hev *enabled* him to distinguish hisself fer superyer ability. Now, as I sed before, I'm a lineal descendant uv ther notorious Ain and Cable, and I've lit down hyar among ye ter explain a few p'ints 'bout true blessedness and true cussedness.

"Oh! brethern, I tell ye I'm a snorter, I am, when I git a-goin'—a wild screechin' cattymount, right down frum ther sublime spheres up Starkey—ar' a regular epizootic uv religyun, sent down frum clouddum and scattered permiscously ter ther forty winds uv ther earth."

We pass the "cattymount," and presently come to a table at which a young and handsome "pilgrim," and a ferret-eyed sharp are engaged at cards. The first mentioned is a tall, robust fellow, somewhere in the neighborhood of twenty-three years of age, with clear-cut features, dark lustrous eyes, and teeth of pearly whiteness. His hair is long and curling, and a soft brown mustache, waxed at the ends, is almost perfection itself.

Evidently he is of quick temperament, for he handles the cards with a swift, nervous dexterity that surprises even the professional sharp himself, who is a black, swarthy-looking customer, with "villain" plainly written in every lineament of his countenance; his eyes, hair, and a tremendous mustache that he occasionally strokes, are of a jetty black; did you ever notice it?—dark hair and complexion predominate among the gambling fraternity.

Perhaps this is owing to the condition of the souls of some of these characters.

The professional sharp in our case was no exception to the rule. He was attired in the hight of fashion, and the diamond cluster, inevitably to be found there, was on his shirt front; a jewel of wonderful size and brilliancy.

"Ah! curse the luck!" exclaimed the sharp, slapping down the cards; "you have won again, pilgrim, and I am five hundred out. By the gods, your luck is something astonishing!"

"*Luck!*" laughed the other, coolly: "well, no. I do not call it luck, for I never have luck. We'll call it chance!"

"Just as you say," growled the gambler, bringing forth a new pack. "Chance and luck are then twin companions. Will you continue longer, Mr. — — "

"Redburn," finished the pilgrim.

"Ah! yes—Mr. Redburn, will you continue?"

"I will play as long as there is anything to play for," again finished Mr. R., twisting the waxed ends of his mustache calmly. "Maybe you have got your fill, eh?"

"No; I'll play all night to win back what I have lost."

A youth, attired in buck-skin, and apparently a couple of years younger than Redburn, came sauntering along at this juncture, and seeing an unoccupied chair at one end of the table (for Redburn and the gambler sat at the sides, facing each other), he took possession of it forthwith.

"Hello!" and the sharp swore roundly. "Who told *you* to mix in your lip, pilgrim?"

"Nobody, as I know of. Thought I'd squat right here, and watch your *sleeves*!" was the significant retort, and the youth laid a cocked six-shooter on the table in front of him.

"Go on, gentlemen; don't let me be the means of spoiling your fun."

The gambler uttered a curse, and dealt out the pasteboards.

The youth was watching him intently, with his sharp black eyes.

He was of medium hight, straight as an arrow, and clad in a loose-fitting costume. A broad sombrero was set jauntily upon the left side of his head, the hair of which had been cut close down to the scalp.

His face—a pleasant, handsome, youthful face—was devoid of hirsute covering, he having evidently been recently handled by the barber.

The game between Mr. Redburn and the gambler progressed; the eyes of he whom we have just described were on the card sharp constantly.

The cards went down on the table in vigorous slaps, and at last, Mr. Pilgrim Redburn raked in the stakes.

"Thunder 'n' Moses!" ejaculated the sharp, pulling out his watch—an elegant affair, of pure gold, and studded with diamonds—and laying it forcibly down upon the table.

"There! what will you plank on that!"

Redburn took up the time-piece, turned it over and over in his hands, opened and shut it, gave a glance at the works, and then handed it over to the youth, whom he instinctively felt was his friend. Redburn had come from the East to dig gold, and therefore was a stranger in Deadwood.

"What is its money value?" he asked, familiarizing his tone. "Good, I suppose."

"Yes, perfectly good, and cheap at two hundred," was the unhesitating reply. "Do you lack funds, stranger?"

"Oh! no. I am three hundred ahead of this cuss yet, and—"

"You'd better quit where you are!" said the other, decisively. "You'll lose the next round, mark my word."

"Ha! ha!" laughed Redburn, who had begun to show symptoms of recklessness. "I'll take my chances. Here, you gamin, I'll cover the watch with two hundred dollars."

Without more ado the stakes were planked, the cards dealt, and the game began.

The youth, whom we will call Ned Harris, was not idle.

He took the revolvers from the table, changed his position so that his face was just in the opposite direction of what it had been, and commenced to pare his finger nails. The fingers were as white and soft as any girl's. In his hand he also held a strangely-angled little box, the sides of which were mirror-glass. Looking at his finger-nails he also looked into the mirror, which gave a complete view of the card-sharp, as he sat at the table.

Swiftly progressed the game, and no one could fail to see how it was going by watching the cunning light in the gambler's eye. At last the game-card went down, and next instant, after the sharp had raked in his stakes, a cocked revolver in either hand of Ned Harris covered the hearts of the two players.

"Hello!" gasped Redburn, quailing under the gaze of a cold steel tube—"what's the row, now?"

"Draw your revolver!" commanded Harris, sternly, having an eye on the card-sharp at the same time, "Come! don't be all night about it!"

Redburn obeyed; he had no other choice.

"Cock it and cover your man!"

"Who do you mean?"

"The cuss under my left-hand aim."

Again the "pilgrim" felt that he could not afford to do otherwise than obey.

So he took "squint" at the gambler's left breast after which Harris withdrew the siege of his left weapon, although he still covered the young Easterner, the same. Quietly he moved around to where the card-sharp sat, white and trembling.

"Gentlemen!" he yelled, in a clear, ringing voice, "will some of you step this way a moment?"

A crowd gathered around in a moment: then the youth resumed:

"Feller-citizens, all of you know how to play cards, no doubt. What is the penalty of cheating, out here in the Hills?"

For a few seconds the room was wrapt in silence; then a chorus of voices gave answer, using a single word:

"Death!"

"Exactly," said Harris, calmly. "When a sharp hides cards in Chinaman fashion up his sleeve, I reckon that's what you call cheatin', don't you?"

"That's the size of it," assented each bystander, grimly.

Ned Harris pressed his pistol-muzzle against the gambler's forehead, inserted his fingers in each of the capacious sleeves, and a moment later laid several high cards upon the table.

A murmur of incredulity went through the crowd of spectators. Even "pilgrim" Redburn was astonished.

After removing the cards, Ned Harris turned and leveled his revolver at the head of the young man from the East.

"Your name?" he said, briefly, "is—"

"Harry Redburn."

"Very well. Harry Redburn, that gambler under cover of your pistol is guilty of a crime, punishable in the Black Hills by death. As you are his victim—or, rather, were to be—it only remains for you to aim straight and rid your country of an A No. 1 dead-beat and swindler!"

"Oh! no!" gasped Redburn, horrified at the thought of taking the life of a fellow-creature—"I cannot, I cannot!"

"You *can*!" said Harris, sternly; "go on—*you must salt that card-sharp, or I'll certainly salt you!*"

A deathlike silence followed.

"*One!*" said Harris, after a moment.

Redburn grew very pale, but not paler was he than the card-sharp just opposite. Redburn was no coward; neither was he accustomed to the desperate character of the population of the Hills. Should he shoot the tricky wretch before him, he knew he should be always calling himself a murderer. On the contrary, in the natural laws of Deadwood, such a murder would be classed justice.

"*Two!*" said Ned Harris, drawing his pistol-hammer back to full cock. "Come, pilgrim, are you going to shoot?"

Another silence; only the low breathing of the spectators could be heard.

"Three!"

Redburn raised his pistol and fired—blindly and carelessly, not knowing or caring whither went the compulsory death-dealing bullet.

There was a heavy fall, a groan of pain, as the gambler dropped over on the floor; then for the space of a few seconds all was the wildest confusion throughout the mammoth saloon.

Revolvers were in every hand, knives flashed in the glare of the lamplight, curses and threats were in scores of mouths, while some of the vast surging crowd cheered lustily.

At the table Harry Redburn still sat, as motionless as a statue, the revolver still held in his hand, his face white, his eyes staring.

There he remained, the center of general attraction, with a hundred pair of blazing eyes leveled at him from every side.

"Come!" said Ned Harris, in a low tone, tapping him on the shoulder—"come, pardner; let's git out of this, for times will be brisk soon. You've wounded one of the biggest card-devils in the Hills, and he'll be rearin' pretty quick. Look! d'ye see that feller comin' yonder, who was preachin' from on top of the barrel, a bit ago? Well, that is Catamount Cass, an' he's a pard of Chet Diamond, the feller you salted, an' them fellers behind him are his gang. Come! follow me, Henry, and I'll nose our way out of here."

Redburn signified his readiness, and with a cocked six-shooter in either hand Ned Harris led the way.

CHAPTER IV.

SAD ANITA—THE MINE LOCATER—TROUBLE

Straight toward the door of the saloon he marched, the muzzles of the grim sixes clearing a path to him; for Ned Harris had become notorious in Deadwood for his coolness, courage and audacity. It had been said of him that he would "just es lief shute a man as ter look at 'im," and perhaps the speaker was not far from right.

Anyway, he led off through the savage-faced audience with a composure that was remarkable, and, strange to say, not a hand was raised to stop him until he came face to face with Catamount Cass and his gang; here was where the youth had expected molestation and hindrance, if anywhere.

Catamount Cass was a rough, illiterate "tough" of the mountain species, and possessed more brute courage than the general run of his type of men, and a bull-dog determination that made him all the more dangerous as an enemy.

Harry Redburn kept close at Ned Harris' heels, a cocked "six" in either hand ready for any emergency.

It took but a few moments before the two parties met, the "Cattymount" throwing out his foot to block the path.

"Hello!" roared the "tough," folding his huge knotty arms across his partially bared breast; "ho! ho! whoa up thar, pilgrims! Don' ye go ter bein' so fast. Fo'kes harn't so much in a hurry now-'days as they uster war. Ter be sure ther Lord manyfactered this futstool in seven days; sum times I think he did, an' then, ag'in, my geological ijees convince me he didn't."

"What has that to do with us?" demanded Ned, sternly. "I opine ye'd better spread, some of you, if you don't want me to run a canyon through your midst. Preach to some other pilgrim than me; I'm in a hurry!"

"Haw! haw! Yas, I observe ye be; but if ye're my meat, an' I think prob'ble ye be, I ain't a-goin' fer ter let yer off so nice and easy.

P'arps ye kin tell who fired the popgun, a minnit ago, w'at basted my ole pard?"

"I shall not take trouble to tell!" replied Ned, fingering the trigger of his left six uneasily. "Ef you want to know who salted Chet Diamond, the worst blackleg, trickster and card-player in Dakota, all you've got to do is to go and ask him!"

"Hold!" cried Harry Redburn, stepping out from behind Harris; "I'll hide behind no man's shoulder. *I* salted the gambler—if you call shooting salting—and I'm not afraid to repeat the action by salting a dozen more just of his particular style."

Ned Harris was surprised.

He had set Redburn down as a faint-hearted, dubious-couraged counter-jumper from the East; he saw now that there was something of him, after all.

"Come on, young man!" and the young miner stepped forward a pace; "are you with me?"

"To the ears!" replied Harris, grimly.

The next instant the twain leaped forward and broke the barrier, and mid the crack of pistol-shots and shouts of rage, they cleared the saloon. Once outside, Ned Harris led the way.

"Come along!" he said, dodging along the shadowy side of the street; "we'll have to scratch gravel, for them up-range 'toughs' will follow us, I reckon. They're a game gang, and 'hain't the most desirable kind of enemies one could wish for. I'll take you over to my coop, and you can lay low there until this jamboree blows over. You'll have to promise me one thing, however, ere I can admit you as a member of my household."

"Certainly. What is it?" and Harry Redburn redoubled his efforts in order to keep alongside his swift-footed guide.

"Promise me that you will divulge nothing, no matter what you may see or hear. Also that, should you fall in love with one who is a member of my family, you will forbear and not speak of love to her."

"It is a woman, then?"

"Yes—a young lady."

"I will promise;—how can I afford to do otherwise, under the existing circumstances. But, tell me, why did you force me to shoot that gambler?"

"He was a rascal, and cheated you."

"I know; but I did not want his life; I am averse to bloodshed."

"So I perceived, and that made me all the more determined you should salivate him. You'll find before you're in the Hills long that it won't do to take lip or lead from any one. A green pilgrim is the first to get salted; I illustrated how to serve 'em!"

Redburn's eyes sparkled. He was just beginning to see into the different phases of this wild exciting life.

"Good!" he exclaimed, warmly. "I have much to thank you for. Did I kill that card-sharp?"

"No; you simply perforated him in the right side. This way."

They had been running straight up the main street. Now they turned a corner and darted down one that was dark and deserted.

A moment later a trim boyish figure stepped before them, from out of the shadow of a new frame building; a hand of creamy whiteness was laid upon the arm of Ned Harris.

"This way, pilgrims," said a low musical voice, and at the same instant a gust of wind lifted the jaunty sombrero from the speaker's head, revealing a most wonderful wealth of long glossy hair; "the 'toughs' are after you, and you cannot find a better place to coop than in here." The soft hand drew Ned Harris inside the building, which was finished, but unoccupied, and Redburn followed, nothing loth to get into a place of safety. So far, Deadwood had not impressed him favorably as being the most peaceable city within the scope of a continent.

Into an inner room of the building they went, and the door was closed behind them. The apartment was small and smelled of green lumber. A table and a few chairs comprised the furniture; a dark lantern burned suspended from the ceiling by a wire. Redburn eyed the strange youth as he and Harris were handed seats.

Of medium hight and symmetrically built; dressed in a carefully tanned costume of buck-skin, the vest being fringed with the fur of the mink; wearing a jaunty Spanish sombrero; boots on the dainty feet of patent leather, with tops reaching to the knees; a face slightly sun-burned, yet showing the traces of beauty that even excessive dissipation could not obliterate; eyes black and piercing; mouth firm, resolute, and devoid of sensual expression: hair of raven color and of remarkable length;—such was the picture of the youth as beheld by Redburn and Harris.

"You can remain here till you think it will be safe to again venture forth, gentlemen," and a smile—evidently a stranger there—broke out about the speaker's lips. "Good-evening!" "Good-evening!" nodded Harris, with a quizzical stare. The next moment the youth was gone.

"Who was that chap?" asked Redburn, not a little bewildered.

"That?—why that's Calamity Jane!"

"Calamity Jane? *What* a name."

"Yes, she's an odd one. Can ride like the wind, shoot like a sharp-shooter, and swear like a trooper. Is here, there and everywhere, seemingly all at one time. Owns this coop and two or three other lots in Deadwood; a herding ranch at Laramie, an interest in a paying placer claim near Elizabeth City, and the Lord only knows how much more."

"But it is not a *woman?*"

"Reckon 'tain't nothin' else."

"God forbid that a child of mine should ever become so debased and—"

"Hold! there are yet a few redeeming qualities about her. She was *ruined*—" and here a shade dark as a thunder-cloud passed over Ned Harris' face—"and set adrift upon the world, homeless and friendless; yet she has bravely fought her way through the storm, without asking anybody's assistance. True, she may not now have a heart; that was trampled upon, years ago, but her character has not suffered blemish since the day a foul wretch stole away her honor!"

"What is her real name?"

"I do not know; few in Deadwood do. It is said, however, that she comes of a Virginia City, Nevada, family of respectability and intelligence."

At this juncture there was a great hubbub outside, and instinctively the twain drew their revolvers, expecting that Catamount Cass and his toughs had discovered their retreat, and were about to make an attack. But soon the gang were beard to tramp away, making the night hideous with their hoarse yells.

"They'll pay a visit to every shanty in Deadwood," said Harris, with a grim smile, "and if they don't find us, which they won't, they'll h'ist more than a barrel of bug-juice over their defeat. Come, let's be going."

They left the building and once more emerged onto the darkened street, Ned taking the lead.

"Follow me, now," he said, tightening his belt, "and we'll get home before sunrise, after all."

He struck out up the gulch, or, rather, down it, for his course lay southward. Redburn followed, and in fifteen minutes the lights of Deadwood—magic city of the wilderness—were left behind. Harris led the way along the rugged mountain stage-road, that, after leaving Deadwood on its way to Camp Crook and Custer City in the south, runs alternately through deep, dark canyons and gorges, with an ease and rapidity that showed him to be well acquainted with the route. About three miles below Deadwood he struck a trail through a transverse canyon running north-west, through which flowed a small stream, known as Brown's creek. The bottom was level and smooth, and a brisk walk of a half-hour brought them to where a horse was tied to an alder sapling.

"You mount and ride on ahead until you come to the end of the canyon," said Harris, untying the horse. "I will follow on after you, and be there almost as soon as you."

Redburn would have offered some objections, but the other motioned for him to mount and be off, so he concluded it best to obey.

The animal was a fiery one, and soon carried him out of sight of Ned, whom he left standing in the yellow moonlight. Sooner than he expected the gorge came to an abrupt termination in the face of a stupendous wall of rock, and nothing remained to do but wait for young Harris.

He soon came, trotting leisurely up, only a trifle flushed in countenance.

"This way!" he said, and seizing the animal by the bit he led horse and rider into a black, gaping fissure in one side of the canyon, that had hitherto escaped Redburn's notice. It was a large, narrow, subterranean passage, barely large enough to admit the horse and rider. Redburn soon was forced to dismount and bring up the rear.

"How far do we journey in this shape?" he demanded, after what seemed to him a long while.

"No further," replied Ned, and the next instant they emerged into a small, circular pocket in the midst of the mountains—one of those beauteous flower-strewn valleys which are often found in the Black Hills.

This "pocket," as they are called, consisted of perhaps fifty acres, walled in on every side by rugged mountains as steep, and steeper, in some places, than a house-roof. On the western side Brown's creek had its source, and leaped merrily down from ledge to ledge into the valley, across which it flowed, sinking into the earth on the eastern side, only to bubble up again, in the canyon, with renewed strength.

The valley was one vast, indiscriminate bed of wild, fragrant flowers, whose volume of perfume was almost sickening when first greeting the nostrils. Every color and variety imaginable was here, all in the most perfect bloom. In the center of the valley stood a log-cabin, overgrown with clinging vines. There was a light in the window, and Harris pointed toward it, as, with young Redburn, he emerged from the fissure.

"There's my coop, pilgrim. There you will be safe for a time, at least." He unsaddled the horse and set it free to graze.

Then they set off down across the slope, arriving at the cabin in due time.

The door was open; a young woman, sweet, yet sad-faced, was seated upon the steps, fast asleep.

Redburn gave an involuntary cry of incredulity and admiration as his eyes rested upon the picture—upon the pure, sweet face, surrounded by a wealth of golden, glossy hair, and the sylph-like form, so perfect in every contour. But a charge of silence from Harris, made him mute.

The young man knelt by the side of the sleeping girl and imprinted a kiss upon the fresh, unpolluted lips, which caused the sleeping beauty to smile in her dreams.

A moment later, however, she opened her eyes and sprung to her feet with a startled scream.

"Oh, Ned!" she gasped, trembling, as she saw him, "how you frightened me. I had a dream—oh, such a sweet dream! and I thought *he* came and kissed—"

Suddenly did she stop as, for the first time, her penetrating blue eyes rested upon Harry Blackburn.

A moment she gazed at him as in a sort of fascination; then, with a low cry, began to retreat, growing deathly pale. Ned Harris stepped quickly forward and supported her on his arm.

"Be calm, Anita," he said, in a gentle, reassuring tone. "This is a young gentleman whom I have brought here to our home for a few days until it will be safe for him to be seen in Deadwood. Mr. Redburn, I make you acquainted with Anita."

A courteous bow from Redburn, a slight inclination of Anita's head, and the introduction was made. A moment later the three entered the cabin, a model of neatness and primitive luxury.

"How is it that you are up so early, dear?" young Harris asked, as he unbuckled his belt and hung it upon a peg in the wall. "You are rarely as spry, eh?"

"Indeed! I have not been to bed at all," replied the girl, a weary smile wreathing her lips. "I was nervous, and feared something was going to happen, so I staid up."

"Your old plea—the presentiment of coming danger, I suppose," and the youth laughed, gayly. "But you need not fear. No one will invade our little Paradise, right away. What is your opinion of it, Redburn?"

"I should say not. I think this little mountain retreat is without equal," replied Harry, with enthusiasm. "The only wonder is, how did you ever stumble into such a delightful place."

"Of that I will perhaps tell you, another time," said Harris, musingly.

Day soon dawned over the mountains, and the early morning sunlight fell with charming effect into the little "pocket," with its countless thousands of odorous flowers, and the little ivy-clad cabin nestling down among them all.

Sweet, sad-faced Anita prepared a sumptuous morning repast out of antelope-steak and the eggs of wild birds, with dainty side dishes of late summer berries, and a large luscious melon which had been grown on a cultivated patch, contiguous to the cabin.

Both Harris and his guest did ample justice to the meal, for they had neither eaten anything since the preceding noon. When they had finished, Ned arose from the table, saying: "Pardner, I shall leave you here for a few days, during which time I shall probably be mostly away on business. Make yourself at home and see that Anita is properly protected; I will return in a week at the furthest;—perhaps in a day or two."

He took down his rifle and belt from the wall, buckled on the latter, and half an hour later left the "pocket." That was a day of days to Harry Redburn. He rambled about the picturesque little valley, romped on the luxuriant grass and gathered wild flowers, alternately. At night he sat in the cabin door and listened to the cries of the night birds and the incessant hooting of the mountain owls (which by the way, are very abundant throughout the Black Hills.)

All efforts to engage Anita in conversation proved fruitless.

On the following day both were considerably astonished to perceive that there was a stranger in their Paradise;—a bow-legged, hump-backed, grisly little old fellow, who walked with a staff. He approached the cabin, and Redburn went out to find who he was.

"Gude-mornin'!" nodded General Nix, (for it was he) with a grin. "I jes' kim over inter this deestrict ter prospect fer gold. Don' seem ter recognize yer unkle, eh? boy; I'm Nix Walsingham Nix, Esquire, geological surveyor an' mine-locater. I've located more nor forty thousan' mines in my day, more or less—ginerally a consider'ble more of less than less of more. I perdict frum ther geological formation o' this nest an' a dream I hed last night, thet thar's sum uv ther biggest veins right in this yere valley as ye'll find in ther Hills!"

"Humph! no gold here," replied Redburn, who had already learned from study and experience how to guess a fat strike. "It is out of the channel."

"No; et's right in the channel."

"Well, I'll not dispute you. How did you get into the valley?"

"Through ther pass," and the General chuckled approvingly. "See'd a feller kim down ther canyon, yesterday, so I nosed about ter find whar he kim from, that's how I got here; 'sides, I hed a dream about this place."

"Indeed!" Redburn was puzzled how to act under the circumstances. Just then there came a piercing scream from the direction of the cabin.

What could it mean? Was Nix an enemy, and was some one else of his gang attacking Anita?

Certainly she *was* in trouble!

CHAPTER V.

SITTING BULL—THE FAIR CAPTIVE.

Fearless Frank stepped back aghast, as he saw the inhuman chief of the Sioux—the cruel, grim-faced warrior, Sitting Bull; shrunk back, and laid his hand upon the butt of a revolver.

"Ha!" he articulated, "is that you, chief? You, and at such work as this?" there was stern reproach in the youth's tone, and certain it is that the Sioux warrior heard the words spoken.

"My friend, Scarlet Boy, is keen with the tongue," he said, frowning. "Let him put shackles upon it, before it leaps over the bounds of reason."

"I see no reason why I should not speak in behalf of yon suffering girl!" retorted the youth, fearlessly, "on whom you have been inflicting one of the most inhuman tortures Indian cunning could conceive. For shame, chief, that you should ever assent to such an act—lower yourself to the grade of a dog by such a dastard deed. For shame, I say!"

Instantly the form of the great warrior straightened up like an arrow, and his painted hand flew toward the pistols in his belt.

But the succeeding second he seemed to change his intention; his hand went out toward the youth in greeting:

"The Scarlet Boy is right," he said, with as much graveness as a red-skin can conceive. "Sitting Bull listens to his words as he would to those of a brother. Scarlet Boy is no stranger in the land of the Sioux; he is the friend of the great chief and his warriors. Once when the storm-gods were at war over the pine forests and picture rocks of the Hills; when the Great Spirit was sending fiery messengers down in vivid streaks from the skies, the Big Chief cast a thunderbolt in playfulness at the feet of Sitting Bull. The shock of the hand of the Great Spirit did not escape me; for hours I lay like one slain in battle. My warriors were in consternation; they ran hither and thither in affright, calling on the Manitou to preserve their chief. You came, Scarlet Boy, in the midst of all the panic;—came, and though then but a stripling, you applied simple remedies that restored Sitting Bull to the arms of his warriors.[A]

"From that hour Sitting Bull was your friend—is your friend, now, and will be as long as the red-men exist as a tribe."

"Thank you, chief;" and Fearless Frank grasped the Indian's hand and wrung it warmly. "I believe you mean all you say. But I am surprised to find you engaged at such work as this. I have been told that Sitting Bull made war only on warriors—not on women."

An ugly frown darkened the savage's face—a frown wherein was depicted a number of slumbering passions.

"The pale-face girl is the last survivor of a train that the warriors of Sitting Bull attacked in Red Canyon. Sitting Bull lost many warriors; yon pale squaw shot down full a half-score before she could be captured; she belongs to the warriors of Sitting Bull, and not to the great chief himself."

"Yet you have the power to free her—to yield her up to me. Consider, chief; are you not enough my friend that you can afford to give me the pale-face girl? Surely, she has been tortured sufficiently to satisfy your braves' thirst for vengeance."

Sitting Bull was silent.

"What will the Scarlet Boy do with the fair maiden of his tribe?"

"Bear her to a place of safety, chief, and care for her until I can find her friends—probably she has friends in the East."

"It shall be as he says. Sitting Bull will withdraw his braves and Scarlet Boy can have the red-man's prize."

A friendly hand-shake between the youth and the Sioux chieftain, a word from the latter to the grim painted warriors, and the next instant the glade was cleared of the savages.

Fearless Frank then hastened to approach the insensible captive, and, with a couple sweeps of his knife, cut the bonds that held her to the torture-stake. Gently he laid her on the grass, and arranged about her half-nude form the garments Sitting Bull's warriors had torn off, and soon he had the satisfaction of seeing her once more clothed properly. It still remained for him to restore her to consciousness, and this promised to be no easy task, for she was in a dead swoon. She was even more beautiful of face and figure than one would have imagined at a first glance. Of a delicate blonde complexion, with pink-tinged cheeks, she made a very pretty picture, her face framed as it was in a wild disheveled cloud of auburn hair.

A hatful of cold water from a neighboring spring dashed into her upturned face; a continued chafing of the pure white soft hands; then there was a convulsive twitching of the features, a low moan, and the eyes opened and darted a glance of affright into the face of the Scarlet Boy.

"Fear not, miss;" and the youth gently supported her to a sitting posture. "I am a friend, and your cruel captors have vamosed. Lucky I came along just as I did, or it's likely they'd have killed you."

"Oh! sir, how can I ever thank you for rescuing me from those merciless fiends!" and the maiden gave him a grateful glance. "They whipped me, terribly!"

"I know, lady—all because you defended yourself in Red Canyon."

"I suppose so: but how did you find out so much, and, also, effect my release from the savages?"

Fearless Frank leaned up against the tree which had been used as the torture-stake, and related what is already known to the reader.

When he had finished, the rescued captive seized his hand between both her own, and thanked him warmly.

"Had it not been for you, sir, no one but our God knows what would have been my fate. Oh! sir, what can I do, more than to thank you a thousand times, to repay you for the great service you have rendered me?"

"Nothing, lady; nothing that I think of at present. Was it not my duty, while I had the power, to free you from the hands of those barbarians? Certainly it was, and I deserve no thanks. But tell me, what is your name, and were your friends all killed in the train from which you were taken?"

"I had no friends, sir, save a lady whose acquaintance I made on the journey out from Cheyenne. As to my name—you can call me Miss Terry."

"Mystery!" in blank amazement.

"Yes;" with a gay laugh—"Mystery, if you choose. My name is Alice Terry."

"Oh!" and the youth began to brighten. "Miss Terry, to be sure; Mystery! ha! ha! good joke. I shall call you the latter. Have you friends and relatives East?"

"No. I came West to meet my father, who is somewhere in the Black Hills."

"Do you know at what place?"

"I do not."

"I fear it will be a hard matter to find him, then. The Hills now have a floating population of about twenty-five thousand souls. Your father would be one to find out of that lot."

A faint smile came over the girl's face. "I should know papa among fifty thousand, if necessary;" she said, "although I have not seen him for years."

She failed to mention how many, or what peculiarities she would recognize him by. Was he blind, deaf or dumb?

Fearless Frank glanced around him, and saw that a path rugged and steep led up to the prairie above.

"Come," he said, offering his arm, "we will get up to the plains and go."

"Where to?" asked Miss Terry, rising with an effort. The welts across her back were swollen and painful.

"Deadwood is my destination. I can deviate my course, however, if it will accommodate you."

"Oh! no; you must not inconvenience yourself on my account. I am of little or no consequence, you know."

She leaned upon his arm, and they ascended the path to the plain above.

Frank's horse was grazing near by where the scarlet youth had taken his unceremonious tumble.

Off to the north-west a cloud of dust rose heavenward, and he rightly conjectured that it hid from view the chieftain, Sitting Bull, and his warriors.

His thoughts reverting to his companion, "General" Nix, and the train of Charity Joe, he glanced toward where he had last seen them.

Neither were to be seen, now. Probably Nix had rejoined the train, and it was out of eye-shot behind a swell in the plains.

"Were you looking for some one?" Alice asked, looking into her rescuer's face.

"Yes, I was with a train when I first heard your cries; I left the boys, and came to investigate. I guess they have gone on without me."

"How mean of them! Will we have to make the journey to the Hills alone?"

"Yes, unless we should providentially fall in with a train or be overtaken by a stage."

"Are you not afraid?"

"My cognomen is Fearless Frank, lady; you can draw conclusions from that."

He went and caught the horse, arranged a blanket in the saddle so that she could ride side-fashion, and assisted her to mount.

The sun was touching the lips of the horizon with a golden kiss; more time than Frank had supposed' had elapsed since he left the train.

Far off toward the east shadows were hugging close behind the last lingering rays of sunlight; a couple of coyotes were sneaking into view a few rods away; birds were winging homeward; a perfume-laden breeze swept down from the Black Hills, and fanned the pink cheeks of Alice Terry into a vivid glow.

"We cannot go far," said Frank, thoughtfully, "before darkness will overtake us. Perhaps we had better remain in the canal, here, where there is both grass and water. In the morning we will take a fresh start."

The plan was adopted; they camped in the break, or "canal," near where Alice had been tortured.

Out of his saddle-bags Frank brought forth crackers, biscuit and dried venison; these, with clear sparkling water from the spring in the chaparral, made a meal good enough for anybody.

The night was warm; no fire was needed.

A blanket spread on the grass served as a resting-place for Alice; the strange youth in scarlet lay with his head resting against the side of his horse. The least movement of the animal, he said, would arouse him; he was keen of scent and quick to detect danger—meaning the horse.

The night passed away without incident; as early as four o'clock— when it is daylight on the plains—Fearless Frank was astir.

Be found the rivulet flowing from the spring to abound with trout, and caught and dressed the morning meal.

Alice was awake by the time breakfast was ready. She bathed her face and hands in the stream, combed her long auburn hair through her fingers, and looked sweeter than on the previous night—at least, so thought Fearless Frank.

"The day promises to be delightful, does it not?" she remarked, as she seated herself to partake of the repast.

"Exactly. Autumn months are ever enjoyable in the West."

The meal dispatched, no delay was made in leaving the place.

Fearless Frank strode along beside his horse and its fair rider, chatting pleasantly, and at the same time making a close observation of his surroundings. He knew he was in parts frequented by both red and white savages, and it would do no harm to keep on one's guard.

They traveled all day and reached Sage creek at sunset.

Here they remained over night, taking an early start on the succeeding morning.

That day they made good progress, in consequence of Frank's purchase of a horse at Sage creek from some friendly Crow Indians, and darkness overtook them at the mouth of Red Canyon, where they went into camp.

By steady pushing they reached Rapid creek the next night, for no halt was made at Custer City, and for the first time since leaving the torture-ground, camped with a miner's family. As yet no cabins or shanties had been erected here, canvas tents serving in the stead; to-day there are between fifty and a hundred wooden structures.

Alice was charmed with the wild grandeur of the mountain scenery—with the countless acres of blossoms and flowering shrubs—with the romantic and picturesque surroundings in general, and was very emphatic in her praises.

One day of rest was taken at Rapid Creek; then the twain pushed on, and when night again overtook them, they rode into the bustling, noisy, homely metropolis—Deadwood, magic city of the North-west.

CHAPTER VI.

ONLY A SNAKE—LOCATING A MINE.

Harry Redburn hurried off toward the cabin, which was some steps away. In Anita's scream there were both terror and affright.

Walsingham Nix, the hump-backed, bow-legged explorer and prospecter hobbled after him, using his staff for support.

He had heard the scream, but years' experience among the "gals" taught him that a feminine shriek rarely, if ever, meant anything.

Redburn arrived at the cabin in a few flying bounds, and leaped into the kitchen.

There, crouched upon the floor in one corner, all in a little heap, pale, tumbling and terrified, was Anita. Before her, squirming along over the sand-scrubbed floor, evidently disabled by a blow, was an enormous black-snake.

It was creeping away instead of toward Anita, leaving a faint trail of crimson in its wake; yet the young girl's face was blanched with fear.

"You screamed at that?" demanded Redburn, pointing to the coiling serpent.

"Ugh! yes; it is horrible."

"But, it is harmless. See: some one has given it a blow across the back, and it is disabled for harm."

Anita looked up into his handsome face, wonderingly.

"I guv et a rap across the spinal column, when I kim into the valley," said General Nix, thrusting his head in at the door, a ludicrous grin elongating his grisly features. "'Twar a-goin' ter guv me a yard or so uv et's tongue, more or less—consider'bly less of more than more of less—so I jest salivated it across ther back, kerwhack!"

Anita screamed again as she saw the General, he was so rough and homely.

"Who are you?" she managed to articulate as Redburn assisted her to rise from the floor. "What are you doing here, where you were not invited?"

There was a degree of haughtiness in her tone that Redburn did not dream she possessed.

The "General" rubbed the end of his nose, chuckled audibly, then laughed, outright.

"I opine this ar' a free country, ain't it, marm, more or less? When a feller kerflummuxes rite down onter a payin' streek I opine he's goin' ter roost that till he gits reddy to vamoose, ain't he?"

"But, sir, my brother was the first to discover this spot and build us a home here, and he claims that all belongs to him."

"He do? more or less—consider'bly less of more than more uv less, eh? Yas, I kno' yer brother—leastways hev seen him an' heerd heeps about him. Letters uv his name spell Ned Harris, not?"

"Yes, sir; but how can you know him? Few do, in Deadwood."

"Nevyer mind that, my puss. Ole Walsingham Nix do kno' a few things yet, ef he ar' a hard old nut fer w'ich thar is not cra'kin'."

Anita looked at Redburn, doubtfully.

"Brother would be very angry if he were to return and find this man here, what would you advise?"

"I am of the opinion that he will have to vacate," replied Harry, decidedly.

"*Nix* cum-a-rouse!" disagreed the old prospecter. "I'm hayr, an' thar's no yearthly use o' denyin *that*. Barrin' ye ar' a right peart-lookin' kid, stranger, allow me ter speculate thet it would take a dozen, more or less—consider'bly less uv more than more o' less— ter put me out."

Redburn laughed heartily. The old fellow's bravado amused him. Anita however, was silent; she put dependence in her protector to arrange matters satisfactorily.

"That savors strongly of rebellion," Redburn observed, sitting down upon a lounge that stood hard by. "Besides, you have an advantage;

I would not attack you; you are old and unfitted for combat; deformed and unable to do battle."

"Exactly!" the "General" confidently announced.

"What good can come of your remaining here?" demanded Anita.

"Sit down, marm, sit down, an I'll perceed ter divest myself uv w'at little information I've got stored up in my noddle. Ye see, mum, my name's Walsingham Nix, at yer sarvice—Walsingham bein' my great, great grandad's fronticepiece, while Nix war ther hind-wheeler, like nor w'at a he-mule ar' w'en hitched ter a 'schooner.' Ther Nix family were a great one, bet yer false teeth; originated about ther time Joner swallered the whale, down nigh Long Branch, and 've bin handed down frum time ter time till ye behold in me ther last surrivin' pilgrim frum ther ancestral block. Thar was one remarkable pecooliarity about ther Nix family, frum root ter stump, an' ther war, they war nevyer known ter refuse a gift or an advantageous offer; in this respeck they bore a striking resemblance ter the immortell G'orge Washington. G'orge war innercent; he ked never tell a lie. So war our family; they never hed it in their hearts to say *Nix* to an offer uv a good feed or a decoction o' brandy.

"It war a disease—a hereditary affection uv ther hull combined system. The terrible malady attacked me w'en I war an infant prodigy, an' I've nevyer yit see'd thet time when I c'u'd resist the temptation an' coldly say 'nix' w'en a brother pilgrim volunteered ter make a liberal dispensation uv grub, terbarker, or bug-juice. Nix ar' a word thet causes sorrer an' suffering ter scores 'n' scores o' people, more or less—generally more uv less than less o' more—an' tharfore I nevyer feel it my duty, as a Christyun, ter set a bad example w'ich others may foller."

Redburn glanced toward Anita, a quizzical expression upon his genial face.

"I fail to see how that has any reference as to the cause of your stay among us," he observed, amused at the quaint lingo of the prospector.

"Sart'in not, sart'in not! I had just begun ter git thar. I've only bin gi'in' ye a geological ijee uv ther Nix family's formation; I'll now perceed to illustrate more clearly, thr'u' veins an' channels hitherto unexplored, endin' up wi' a reg'lar hoss-car proposal."

Then the old fellow proceeded with a rambling "yarn," giving more guesses than actual information and continued on in this strain:

"So thar *war* gold. I went ter work an' swallered a pill o' opium, w'ich made me sleep, an' while I whar snoozin' I dreampt about ther perzact place whar thet gold war secreted. It war in a little pocket beneath the bed of a spring frum which flowed a little creeklet.

"Next mornin', bright an' early, I shouldered pick, shuvyel an' pan, an' went for thet identical spring. To-day thet pocket, havin' been traced into a rich vein, is payin' as big or bigger nor any claim on Spring creek."[B]

Both Redburn and Anita were unconsciously becoming interested.

"And do you think there is gold here, in this flower-strewn pocket-valley?"

"I don't think it—I know it. I hed a dreem et war hayr in big quantities, so I h'isted my carcass this direction. Ter-nite I'll hev ernuther nighthoss, an' thet'll tell me precisely where ther strike ar'."

Redburn drummed a tattoo on the arm of the lounge his fingers; he was reflecting on what he had heard.

"You are willing to make terms, I suppose," he said, after a while, glancing at Anita to see if he was right. "You are aware, I believe, that we still hold possession above any one else."

"True enuff. Ye war first ter diskiver this place ye orter hev yer say about it."

"Well, then, perhaps we can come to a bargain. You can state your prices for locating and opening up this mine, and we will consider."

"Wal, let me see. Ef the mine proves to be ekal ter the one thet I located on Spring creek, I'll take in a third fer my share uv the divys. Ef 'tain't good's I expect, I'll take a quarter."

Redburn turned to Anita.

"From what little experience I have had, I think it is a fair offer. What is your view of the matter and do you believe your brother will be satisfied?"

"Oh! yes, sir. It will surprise and please him, to return and find his Paradise has been turned into a gold-mine."

"All right; then, we will go ahead and get things to shape. We will have to get tools, though, before we can accomplish much of anything."

"My brother has a miner's outfit here," said Anita. "That will save you a trip to Deadwood, for the present."

And so it was all satisfactorily arranged. During the remainder of the day the old "General" and Redburn wandered about through the flower-meadows of the pocket, here and there examining a little soil now chipping rock among the rugged foothills, then "feeling" in the bed of the creek. But, not a sign of anything like gold was to be found, and when night called them to shelter, Redburn was pretty thoroughly convinced that Nix was an enormous "sell," and that he could put all the gold they would find in his eye. The "General," however, was confident of success, and told many doubtful yarns of former discoveries and exploits.

Anita prepared an evening meal that was both tempting and sumptuous, and all satisfied their appetites after which Harry took down the guitar, suspended from the wall, tuned it up, and sung in a clear mellow voice a number of ballads, to which the "General," much to the surprise of both Redburn and Anita, lent a rich deep bass—a voice of superior culture.

The closing piece was a weird melody—the lament of a heart that was broken, love-blasted—and was rendered in a style worthy of a professional vocalist. The last mournful strains filled the cabin just as the last lingering rays of sunlight disappeared from the mountain top, and shadows came creeping down the rugged walls of rock to concentrate in the Flower Pocket, as Anita had named her valley home. Redburn rose from his seat at the window, and reached the instrument to its accustomed shelf, darting a glance toward sad Anita, a moment later. To his surprise he perceived that her head was bowed upon her arm that lay along the window-ledge—that she was weeping, softly, to herself.

Acting the gentlemanly part, the young miner motioned for Nix to follow him, and they both retired to the outside of the cabin to lounge on the grass and smoke, and thus Anita was left alone with her grief and such troubles as were the causes thereof.

Certain it was that she had a secret, but what it was Redburn could not guess.

About ten o'clock he and Nix re-entered the cabin and went to bed in a room allotted to them, off from the little parlor. Both went to sleep at once, and it was well along toward morning when Redburn was aroused by being rudely shaken by "General" Nix, who was up and dressed, and held a torch in his hand.

"Come! come!" he said in a husky whisper, and a glance convinced Harry that he was still asleep, although his eyes were wide open and staring.

Without a word the young man leaped from bed, donned his garments, and the old man then led the way out of the cabin.

In passing through the kitchen, Redburn saw that Anita was up and waiting.

"Come!" he said, seizing a hatchet and stake, "we are about to discover the gold-mine, and our fortunes;" with a merry laugh.

Then both followed in the wake of the sleep walker, and were led to near the center of the valley, which was but a few steps in the rear of the cabin. Here was a bed of sand washed there from an overflow of the stream, and at this the "General" pointed, as he came to a halt.

"There! *there* is the gold—millions of it deep down—twenty or thirty feet—in sand—easy to get! dig! DIG! DIG!"

Redburn marked the spot by driving the stake in the ground.

It now only remained to dig in the soil to verify the truth of the old man's fancy.

FOOTNOTES:

[A] A fact.

CHAPTER VII.

DEADWOOD DICK ON THE ROAD.

Rumbling noisily through the black canyon road to Deadwood, at an hour long past midnight, came the stage from Cheyenne, loaded down with passengers, and full five hours late, on account of a broken shaft, which had to be replaced on the road. There were six plunging, snarling horses attached, whom the veteran Jehu on the box, managed with the skill of a circusman, and all the time the crack! snap! of his long-lashed gad made the night resound as like so many pistol reports.

The road was through a wild tortuous canyon, fringed with tall spectral pines, which occasionally admitted a bar of ghostly moonlight across the rough road over which the stage tore with wild recklessness.

Inside, the vehicle was crammed full to its utmost capacity, and therefrom emanated the strong fumes of whisky and tobacco smoke, and stronger language, over the delay and the terrible jolting of the conveyance.

In addition to those penned up inside, there were two passengers positioned on top, to the rear of the driver, where they clung to the trunk railings to keep from being jostled off.

One was an elderly man, tall in stature and noticeably portly, with a florid countenance, cold gray eyes, and hair and beard of brown, freely mixed with silvery threads. He was elegantly attired, his costume being of the finest cloth and of the very latest cut: boots patent leathers, and hat glossy as a mirror; diamonds gleamed and sparkled on his immaculate shirt-bosom, on his fingers and from the seal of a heavy gold chain across his vest front.

The other personage was a counterpart of the first to every particular, save that while one was more than a semi-centenarian to years, the other was barely twenty. The same faultless elegance in dress, the same elaborate display of jewels, and the same haughty, aristocratic bearing produced in one was mirrored to the other.

They were father and son.

"Confound such a road!" growled the younger man, as the stage bounced him about like a rubber ball. "For my part I wish I had remained at home, instead of coming out into this outlandish region. It is perfectly awful."

"Y-y-y-e-s!" chattered the elder between the jolts and jerks—"it is not what it should be, that's true. But have patience; ere long we will reach our destination, and—"

"Get shot like poor Vansevere did!" sneered the other. "I tell you, governor, this is a desperate game you are playing."

The old man smiled, grimly.

"Desperate or not, we must carry it through to the end. Vansevere was not the right kind of a man to set after the young scamp."

"How do you mean?"

"He was too rash—entirely too rash. Deadwood Dick is a daring whelp, and Vansevere's open offer of a reward for his apprehension only put the young tiger on his guard, and he will be more wary and watchful in the future."

This in a positive tone.

"Yes; he will be harder to trap than a fox who has lost a foot between jaws of steel. He will be revengeful, too!"

"Bah! I fear him not, old as I am. He is but a boy in years, you remember, and will be easily managed."

"I hope so; I don't want my brains blown out, at least."

The stage rumbled on; the Jehu cursed and lashed his horses; the canyon grew deeper, narrower and darker, the grade slightly descending.

The moon seemed resting on the summit of a peak, hundreds of feet above, and staring down in surprise at the noisy stage.

Alexander Filmore (the elder passenger) succeeded in steadying himself long enough to ignite the end of a cigar to the bowl of Jehu's grimy pipe; then he watched the trees that flitted by. Clarence, his son, had smoked incessantly since leaving Camp Crook, and now threw away his half-used cheroot, and listened to the sighing of the spectral pines.

"The girl—what about her?" he asked, after some moments had elapsed.

"She will be as much to the way as the boy will."

"She? Well, we'll attend to her after we git him out of the way. He is the worst obstacle to our path, at present. Maybe when you see the girl you will take a fancy to her."

"Pish! I want no petticoats clinging to me—much less an ignorant backwoods clodhopper. She is probably a fit mate for an Indian chief."

"You are too rough on the tender sex, boy," and the elder Filmore gave vent to a disconnected laugh. "You must remember that your mother was a woman."

"Was she?" Clarence bit the end of his waxed mustache, and mused over his sire's startling announcement. "*You* recollect that I never saw her."

"D'ye carry poppin'-jays, pilgrims?" demanded Jehu, turning so suddenly upon the two passengers as to frighten them out of their wits.

"Popping-jays?" echoed Filmore, senior.

"Yas—shutin'-irons—rewolvers—patent perforatin' masheens."

"Yes, we are armed, if that is what you mean."

On dashed the stage through the echoing canyon—on plunged the snorting horses, excited to greater efforts by the frequent application of the cracking lash. The pines grew thicker, and the moonlight less often darted its rays down athwart the road.

"Hey!" yelled a rough voice from within the stage "w'at d'ye drive so fast fer? Ye've jonced the senses clean out uv a score o' us."

"Go to blazes!" shouts back Jehu, giving an extra crack to his whip. "Who'n the name o' John Rodgers ar' drivin' this omnybust, pilgrim?—you or I?"

"You'll floor a hoss ef ye don' mind sharp!"

"Who'n thunder wants ye to pay fer et, ef I do?" rings back, tauntingly. "Reckon w'en Bill McGucken can't drive ther thru-ter-Deadwood stage as gude as ther average, he'll suspend bizness, or hire *you* ter steer to his place."

On, on rumbles the stage, down through a lower grade of the canyon, where no moonlight penetrates, and all is of Stygian darkness.

The two passengers on top of the stage shiver with dread, and even old Bill McGucken peers around him, a trifle suspiciously.

It is a wild spot, with the mountains rising on each side of the road to a stupendous hight, the towering pines moaning their sad, eternal requiem; the roar of the great wheels over the hardpan bottom; the snorting of the fractious lead-horses; the curses and the cracking of Jehu's whip; the ring of iron-shod hoofs—it is a place and moment conducive to fear, mute wonder, admiration.

"Halt!"

High above all other sounds now rings this cry, borne toward the advancing stage from the impenetrable space of gloom ahead, brought down in clear commanding tone whereto there is neither fear nor hesitation.

That one word has marvelous effect. It brings a gripe of iron into the hands of Jehu, and he jerks his snorting steeds back upon their haunches; it is instrumental in stopping the stage. (Who ever knew a Black Hills driver to offer to press on when challenged to halt to a wild dismal place?)

It sends a thrill of lonely horror through the vein of those to whose ears the cry is borne; it causes hands to fly to the butts of weapons, and hearts to beat faster.

"Halt!" Again the cry rings forth, reverberating in a hundred dissimilar echoes up the rugged mountain side.

The horses quiet down: Jehu sits like a carved statue on his box; the silence becomes painful to those within the stage—those who are trembling in a fever of excitement, and peering from the open windows with revolvers cocked for instant use.

The moon suddenly thrusts her golden head over the pinnacle of a hoary peak a thousand feet above and lights up the gorge with a ghastly distinctness that enables the watchers to behold a black horseman blocking the path a few rods ahead.

"Silence! Listen!" Two words this time, in the same clear, commanding voice. A pause of a moment, then the stillness is broken by the ominous click! click! of a score of rifles; this alone announces that the stage is "covered."

Then the lone horseman rides leisurely down toward the stage, and Jehu recognizes him. It is Deadwood Dick, Prince of the Road!

Mounted upon his midnight steed, and clad in his weird suit of black, he makes an imposing spectacle, as he comes fearlessly up. Well may he be bold and fearless, for no one dares to raise a hand against him, when the glistening barrels of twelve rifles protruding from each thicket that fringes the road threaten those within and without the stage.

Close up to the side of the coach rides the daring young outlaw, his piercing orbs peering out from the eye-holes in his black mask, one hand clasping the bridle-reins the other a nickel-plated seven-shooter drawn back at full cock.

"You do well to stop, Bill McGucken!" the road-agent, observes, reining in his steed. "I expected you hours ago, on time."

"Twarn't my fault, yer honor!" replies Jehu, meek as a lamb under the gaze of the other's popgun. "Ye see, we broke a pole this side o' Custer City, an' that set us behind several p'ints o' ther compass."

"What have you aboard to-night worth examining!"

"Nothin', yer honor. Only a stageful uv passengers, this trip."

"Bah! you are getting poor. Get down from off the box, there!"

The driver trembled, and hesitated.

"*Get* down!" again commanded the road-agent, leveling his revolver, "before I drop you."

49

In terror McGucken made haste to scramble to the ground, where he stood with his teeth chattering and knees knocking together in a manner pitiable to see. "Ha, ha, ha!" That wild laugh of Deadwood Dick's made the welkin ring out a weird chorus. "Bill McGucken, you should join the regular army, you are so brave. Ha, ha, ha!"

And the laugh was taken up by the road-knights, concealed in the thicket, and swelled into a wild, boisterous shout.

Poor McGucken trembled in his boots in abject terror, while those inside the coach were pretty well scared.

"Driver!" said the Prince of the Road, coolly, after the laugh, "go you to the passengers who grace this rickety shebang and take up a collection. You needn't cum to me wi' less'n five hundred ef ye don't want me to salt ye!"

Bowing humble obeisance, McGucken took off his hat, and made for the stage door.

"Gentlemen!" he plead, "there is need o' yer dutchin' out yer dudads right liberal ef ye've enny purtic'lar anticypation an' desire ter git ter Deadwood ter-night. Dick, the Road-Agent, are law an' gospel heerabouts, I spec'late!"

"Durned a cent'll I fork!" growled one old fellow, loud enough to be heard. "I ain't afeerd o' all the robber Dicks from here ter Jerusalum."

But when he saw the muzzle of the young road-agent's revolver gazing in through the window, he suddenly changed his mind, and laid a plethoric pocketbook into McGucken's already well-filled hat.

The time occupied in making the collection was short, and in a few moments the Jehu handed up his battered "plug" to the Prince of the Road for inspection.

Coolly Deadwood Dick went over the treasure, as if it were all rightfully his own; then he chucked hat and all into one of his saddle-bags, after which he turned his attention toward the stage. As he did so he saw for the first time the two passengers on top, and as he gazed at them a gleam of fire shot into his eyes and his hands nervously griped at his weapon.

"Alexander Filmore, you here!" he ejaculated, his voice betraying his surprise.

"Yes," replied the elder Filmore, coldly—"here to shoot you, you dastardly dog," and quickly raising a pistol, he took rapid and deadly aim, and fired.

FOOTNOTES:

[B] A fact.

CHAPTER VIII.

NOT YET!

With a groan Deadwood Dick fell to the ground, blood spurting from a wound in his breast. The bullet of the elder Filmore had indeed struck home.

Loud then were the cries of rage and vengeance, as a score of masked men poured out from the thickets, and surrounded the stage.

"Shoot the accursed nigger!" cried one. "He's killed our leader, an' by all the saints in ther calendur he shall pay the penalty!"

"No! no!" yelled another, "well do no such a thing. He shall swing in mid-air!"

"Hey!" cried a third, rising from the side of the prostrate load-agent, "don' ye be so fast, boys. The capt'in still lives. He is not seriously wounded even!"

A loud huzza went up from the score of throats, that caused a thousand echoing reverberations along the mountain side.

"Better let ther capt'in say what we shall do wi' yon cuss o' creashun!" suggested one who was apparently a leading spirit; "it's *his* funeral, ain't it?"

"Yas, yas, it's his funeral!"

"Then let him do ther undertakin'."

Robber Dick was accordingly supported to a sitting posture, and the blood that flowed freely from his wound was stanched. In the operation his mask became loosened and slipped to the ground, but so quickly did he snatch it up and replace it, that no one caught even a glimpse of his face.

In the meantime Clarence Filmore had discharged every load in his two six-shooters into the air. He had an object in doing this; he thought that the reports of fire-arms would reach Deadwood (which

52

was only a short mile distant, around the bend), and arouse the military, who would come to his rescue.

Dick's wound dressed, he stood once more upon his feet, and glared up at the two men on the box. They were plainly revealed in the ghostly moonlight, and their features easily studied.

"Alexander Filmore!" the young road-agent said, a terrible depth of meaning in his voice, that the cowering wretch could but understand.

"Alexander Filmore, you have at last come out and shown your true colors. What a treacherous, double-dyed villain you are! Better so; better that you should take the matter into your own hands and face the music, than to employ *tools,* as you have done heretofore. I can fight a dozen enemies face to face better than one or two lurking in the bushes."

The elder Filmore uttered a savage curse.

"You triumph *now!*" he growled, biting his nether lip in vexation; "but it will not always be thus."

"Eh? think not? I think I shall have to *adopt* you for awhile. Boys, haul down the two, and bind them securely."

Accordingly, a rush was made upon the stage, and the two outside passengers. Down they were hauled, head over heels, and quickly secured by strong cords about the wrists and ankles.

This done, Deadwood Dick turned to Bill McGucken, who had ventured to clamber to the seat of the coach.

"Drive on, you cowardly lout—drive on. We've done with you for the present. But, remember, not a word of this to the population of Deadwood, if you intend to ever make another trip over this route. Now, go!"

Jehu needed not the second invitation. He never was tardy in getting out of the way of danger: so he picked up the reins, gave an extra hard crack of the long whip, and away rolled the jolting stage through the black canyon, disappearing a moment later around the bend, beyond which lay Deadwood—magic city of the wilderness.

Then, out from the thicket the road-agents led their horses; the two prisoners were secured in the saddles in front of two brawny outlaws, and without delay the cavalcade moved down the gorge, weirdly illuminated by the mellow rays of the soaring moon.

Clarence Filmore had hoped that the report of his pistol-shots would reach Deadwood. If so, his wishes were fulfilled. The reports reached the barracks above Deadwood just as a horseman galloped up the hill—Major R— —, just in from a carouse down at the "Met."

"Halloo!" he shouted, loudly. "To horse! there is trouble in the gorge. The Sioux, under Sitting Bull, are upon us!"

As the major's word was law at the barracks, in very short order the garrison was aroused, and headed by the major in person, a cavalcade of sleepy soldiers swept down the gorge toward the place whence had come the firing.

Wildly around the abrupt bend they dashed with yells of anticipated victory: then there was a frightful collision between the incoming stage and the outgoing cavalry; the shrieks and screams of horses, the curses and yells of wounded men; and a general pandemonium ensued.

The coach, passengers, horses and all was upset, and went rolling down a steep embankment.

Major R— — was precipitated headlong over the embankment, and in his downward flight probably saw more than one soaring comet. He struck head-first in a muddy run, and a sorrier-looking officer of the U.S.A. was never before seen in the Black Hills as he emerged from his bath, than the major. His ridiculous appearance went so far as to stay the general torrent of blasphemy and turn it into a channel of boisterous laughter.

No delay was made in putting things ship-shape again, and ere morning dawned Deadwood beheld the returned soldiers and wrecked stage with its sullen passengers within its precincts.

Dick and his men rode rapidly down the canyon, the two prisoners bringing up the rear under the escort of two masked guards.

These guards were brothers and Spanish-Mexicans at that.

The elder Filmore, a keen student of character, was not long in making out these Spaniards' true character, nor did their greedy glances toward his and his son's diamonds escape him.

"We want to get free!" he at last whispered, when none of those ahead were glancing back. "You will each receive a cool five hundred apiece if you will set us at liberty."

The two road-agents exchanged glances.

"It's a bargain!" returned one. "Stop your horses, and let the others go on!"

The main party were at this juncture riding swiftly down a steep grade.

The four horses were quietly reined in, and when the others were out of hearing, their noses were turned back up the canyon in the direction of Deadwood.

"This will be an unhealthy job for us!" said one of the brothers, "should we ever meet Dick again."

"Fear him not!" replied Alexander Filmore, with an oath. "If he ever crosses your path shoot him down like a dog, and I'll give you a thousand dollars for the work. The sooner he dies the better I'll be suited."

He spoke in a tone of strongest hate—deepest rancor.

CHAPTER IX.

AT THE "MET."

A few nights subsequent to the events related in our last chapter, it becomes our duty to again visit the notorious "Metropolitan" saloon of Deadwood, to see what is going on there.

As usual everything around the place and in it is literally "red hot." The bars are constantly crowded, the gaming-tables are never empty, and the floor is so full of surging humanity that the dance, formerly a chief attraction, has necessarily been suspended.

The influx of "pilgrims" into the Black Hills for the last few days has been something more than wonderful, every stage coming in overcharged with feverish passengers, and from two to a dozen trains arriving daily.

Of course Deadwood receives a larger share of all this immigration — nothing is more natural, for the young metropolis of the hills is *the* miner's rendezvous, being in the center of the best yielding locates.

Every person in Deadwood can tell you where the "Met" is, as it is general head-quarters.

We mount the mud-splashed steps and disappear behind the screen that stands in front of the door. Then the merry clink of glasses, snatches of ribald song, and loud curses from the polluted lips of some wretch who has lost heavily at the gaming-table, reach our hearing, while our gaze wanders over as motley a crowd as it has ever been our fortune to behold.

Men from the States—lawyers, doctors, speculators, adventurers, pilgrims, and dead-beats; men from the western side of the Missouri; grisly miners from Colorado; hunters and trappers from Idaho and Wyoming; card sharps from Denver and Fr'isco; pickpockets from St. Joe and bummers from Omaha—all are here, each one a part of a strange and on the whole a very undesirable community.

Although the dance has been suspended, that does not necessitate the discharge of the brazen-faced girls, and they may yet be seen here with the rest mingling freely among the crowd.

Seated at a table in a somewhat retired corner, were two persons engaged at cards. One was a beardless youth attired in buck-skin, and armed with knife and pistols; the other a big, burly tough from the upper chain—grisly, bloated and repulsive. He, too, was nothing short of a walking arsenal, and it was plain to see that he was a desperate character.

The game was poker. The youth had won three straight games and now laid down the cards that ended the fourth in his favor.

"You're flaxed ag'in, pardner!" he said, with a light laugh, as he raked in the stakes. "This takes your all, eh?"

"Every darned bit!" said the "Cattymount"—for it was he—with an oath. "You've peeled me to ther hide, an' no mistake. Salivated me' way out o' time, sure's thar ar' modesty in a bar-girl's tongue!"

The youth laughed. "You are not in luck to-night. Maybe your luck will return, if you keep on. Haven't you another V?"

"Nary another!"

"Where's your pard, that got salted the other night?"

"Who—Chet Diamond? Wal, hee's around heer, sum'ars, but I can't borry none off o' him. No; I've gotter quit straight off."

"I'll lend you ten to begin on," said the youth, and he laid an X in the ruffian's hands. "There, now, go ahead with your funeral. It's your deal."

The cards were dealt, and the game played, resulting in the favor of the "Cattymount." Another and another was played, and the tough won every time. Still the youth kept on, a quiet smile resting on his pleasant features, a twinkle in his coal-black eye. The youth, dear reader, you have met before.

He is not he, but instead—Calamity Jane. On goes the game, the burly "tough" winning all the time, his pile of tens steadily increasing in hight.

"Talk about Joner an' the ark, an' Noar an' ther whale!" he cries, slapping another X onto the pile with great enthusiasm; "I hed a grate, grate muther-in-law w'at played keerds wi' Noar inside o' thet eyedentical whale's stummick—played poker wi' w'alebones fer pokers. They were afterward landed at Plymouth rock, or sum uther big rock, an' fit together, side by side, in the rebellyuns."

"Indeed!"—with an amused laugh—"then you must have descended from a long line of respected ancestors."

"Auntsisters? Wa'al, I jest about reckon I do. I hev got ther blood o' Cain and Abel in my veins, boyee, an' ef I ken't raise the biggest kind o' Cain tain't because I ain't *able*—oh! no. Pace anuther pilgrim?"

"I reckon. How much have ye got piled up thar in that heap!"

"Squar' ninety tens, my huckleberry, an' all won fa'r, you bet."

"Then it's the first time you ever won anything fair, Cass Diamond!" exclaimed a voice close hand, and the two players looked up to see Ned Harris standing near by, with his hands clasped across his breast.

Calamity Jane nodded, indifferently. She had seen the young miner on several occasions; once she had been rendered an invaluable service when he rescued her from a brawl in which a dozen toughs had attacked her.

"Cattymount" Cass, brother of Chet Diamond, the Deadwood card-king, recognized him also, and with an oath, sprung to his feet.

"By all the Celestyals!" he ejaculated, jerking forth a six-shooter— "by all the roarin', screechin, shriekin', yowlin', squawkin,' ring-tailed, flat-futted cattymounts thet ever did ther forest aisles o' old Alaska traverse! *you* here, ye infernal smooth-faced varmint? *You* heer, arter all ye've did to ride ther cittyzens o' Deadwood inter rebellyun, ye leetle pigminian deputy uv ther devil? Hurra! hurra! boys; let's string him up ter ther nearest sapling!"

"Hal ha!" laughed Harris, coolly, "hear the coward squeal for his pard's assistance. Dassen't stand on his own leather fer fear of gettin' salted fer all he's worth."

"You're a liar!" roared the "Cattymount" spreading himself about promiscuously, but the two words had scarcely left his lips when a blow from the fist of Ned Harris reached him under the left eye, and he went sprawling on the ground in a heap.

"Here! here!" roared a stranger, rushing in upon the scene, and hurling the crowd aside with a dexterity something wonderful. "What is the meaning of all this? Who knocked Cass Diamond down?"

"I had that honor!" coolly remarked Ned Harris, stepping boldly up and confronting the Deadwood card-king, for it was the notorious Chet Diamond who had asked the question. "I smacked him in the gob, Chet Diamond, for calling me a liar, and am ready to accommodate a few more, if there are any who wish to prefer the same charge!"

"Bully, Ned! and here's what will back you!" cried Calamity Jane, leaping to the miner's side, a cocked six in either white, shapely hand; "so sail in, pilgrims!"

Diamond cowered back, and swore furiously. The wound in his breast was yet sore and rankling, and he knew he owed it to the cool and calculating young miner whose name was an omen of terror among toe "toughs" of Deadwood.

"Come on, you black-hearted ace thief!" shouted Calamity Jane, thrusting the muzzle of one of her plated revolvers forcibly under the gambler's prominent nose—"come on! slide in if you are after squar' up-an'-down fun. We'll greet you, best we know how, an' not charge you anything, either. See! I've got a couple full hands o' sixes—every one's a trump! Ain't ye got no aces hid up yer sleeves?"

The card sharp still cursed furiously, and backed away. He dare not reach for a weapon lest the dare-devil girl or young Harris (who now held a cocked pill-box in each hand),-"should salt him on a full lay."

"Ha! ha! ha!" and the laugh of Calamity rung wildly through the great saloon—"Ha! ha! ha! here's a go! Who wants to buy a cupped-winged sharp?"

"Sold out right cheap!" added Ned, facetiously. "Clear the track and we'll take him out and boost him to a limb."

At this juncture some half a dozen of the gambler's gang came rushing up, headed by Catamount Cass, who had recovered from the effects of the blow from Harris' fist.

"At them! at 'em!" roared the "screechin' cattymount frum up nor'."
"Rip, dig an' gouge 'em. Ho! ho! we'll see now who'll swing, *we* will! We'll l'arn who'll display his agility in mid-air, we will. At 'em, b'yees, at 'em. We'll hang 'em like they do hoss-thieves down at Cheyenne!"

Then followed a pitched battle in the bar-room of the "Metropolitan" saloon, such as probably never occurred there before, and never has since.

Revolvers flashed on every hand, knives clashed in deadly conflict; yells, wild, savage, and awful made a perfect pandemonium, to which was added a second edition in the shape of oaths, curses, and groans. Crack! whiz! bang! the bullets flew about like hailstones, and men fell to the reeking floor each terrible moment.

The two friends were not alone in the affray.

No sooner had Catamount Cass and his gang of "toughs" showed fight, than a company of miners sprung to Harris' side, and showed their willingness to fight it out on the square line.

Therefore, once the first shot was fired, it needed not a word to pitch the battle.

Fiercely waged the contest—now hand to hand—loud rose the savage yells on the still night air.

One by one men fell on either side, their life-blood crimsoning the floor, their dying groans unheeded in the fearful melee.

Still unharmed, and fighting among the first, we see Ned Harris and his remarkable companion, Calamity Jane; both are black, and scarcely recognizable in the cloud of smoke that fills the bar-room. Harris is wounded in a dozen places and weak from loss of blood; yet he stands up bravely and fights mechanically.

Calamity Jane if she is wounded shows it not, but faces the music with as little apparent fear as any of those around her.

On wages the battle, even as furiously as in its beginning; the last shot has been fired; it is now knife to knife, and face to face.

Full as many of one side as the other have fallen, and lay strewn about under foot, unthought of, uncared for in the excitement of the desperate moment. Gallons of blood have made the floor slippery and reeking, so that it is difficult to retain one's footing.

At the head of the ruffians the Diamond brothers[C] still hold sway, fighting like madmen in their endeavors to win a victory. They cannot do less, for to back off in this critical moment means sure death to the weakening party.

But hark! what are these sounds?

The thunder of hoofs is heard outside; the rattle of musketry and sabers, and the next instant a company of soldiery, headed by Major R— —, ride straight up into the saloon, firing right and left.

"Come!" cried Calamity Jane, grasping Harris by the arm, and pulling him toward a side door, "it's time for us to slope now. It's every man for himself."

And only under her guidance was Ned able to escape, and save being tailed and captured with the rest.

About noon of the succeeding day, two persons on horseback were coming along the north gulch leading into Deadwood, at an easy canter. They were the fearless Scarlet Boy, or as he is better known, Fearless Frank, and his lovely protege, Miss Terry. They had been for a morning ride over to a neighboring claim, and were just returning.

Since their arrival in Deadwood the youth had devoted a part of his time in a search for Alice's father, but all to no avail. None of the citizens of Deadwood or its surroundings had ever heard of such a person as Captain Walter Terry.

The young couple had become fast friends from their association, and Alice was improving in looks every day she stayed in the mountains.

"I feel hungry," observed Frank, as they rode along. "This life in the hills gives me a keen appetite. How is it with you, lady?"

"The same as with you, I guess. But look! Yonder comes a horseman toward us!"

It was even so. A horseman was galloping up the gulch—no other than our young friend, Ned Harris.

As the two parties approach, the faces of each of the youths grow deadly pale; there comes into their eyes an ominous glitter; their hands each clasp the butt of a revolver, and they gradually draw rein.

That they are enemies of old—that the fire of rancor burns in their hearts, and that this meeting is unexpected, is plain to see.

Now, that they have met, probably for the first time in months or years, it remains not to be doubted but a settlement must come between them—that their hate must result in satisfaction, whether in blood or not.

CHAPTER X

THE DUEL AND ITS RESULT.

Belligerent were the glances exchanged between the two, as they sat there facing each other, each with a hand closed over the butt of a pistol; each as motionless as a carved statue.

Alice Terry had grown pale, too. She saw that friend and protector and the stranger were enemies,—that this meeting though purely accidental was not to end without trouble. Her lips grew set, her eyes flashed, and she reined her horse closer to that of the Scarlet Boy.

Ned Harris let a faint smile, of contempt and pity combined, come into relief on his lips, as he saw this action. Better ten male enemies than one female, he thought; but, then, women must not stand in the way, now. No! nothing must block the path intervening between enmity and vengeance.

Harris was, if anything, the coolest of the three; but, after all, why should he not be? He had spent several years in society that seemed callous to fear,—that knew not what it was to be a Christian; where the utmost coolness was necessary to the preservation of life; where bravery was all and education a dead letter. Fearless Frank, too, had seen all phases of rough western life, probably, but his temperament was more nervous and excitable, his passions tenfold harder to restrain. Still, he managed to exercise a cool exterior now, that equaled that of his opposite—his hated enemy. Mystery, as Frank habitually called the girl, did not offer to conceal her feelings. It was but natural that she should side with him to whom she owed her life, and the glances of scorn and indignation she shot at the young miner might have driven another man than him into a retreat.

Fearless Frank made no motion toward speech; he was determined that the young miner should open the quarrel, if a quarrel it was to be. But beneath his firm-set lips were clenched two rows of teeth, tightly, fiercely; while every nerve in the youth's body was drawn to its utmost tension.

Harris was wonderfully calm and at ease; only a gray pallor on his handsome face and a menacing fire in his piercing eyes told that he was in the least agitated.

"Justin McKenzie!"

Sternly rung out the words on the clear mountain air. Ned Harris had spoken, and the grayish pallor deepened on his countenance while the fire of rancor burned with stronger gleam in his eagle eye.

The effect on the scarlet youth was scarcely noticeable, more than that the lips grew more rigid and compressed, and the right hand clutched the pistol-butt more tightly. But no answer to the other's summons.

"Justin McKenzie!" again said the young miner, calmly, "do you recognize me?"

The Scarlet Boy bows his head slowly, his eyes watchful lest the other shall catch the drop on him.

"Justin McKenzie, you *do* recognize me, even after the elapse of two long weary years, during which I have sought for you faithfully, but failed to find you until this hour. We have at last met, and the time for settlement between you and me, Justin McKenzie, has arrived. Here in this out-of-the-way gorge, we will settle the grudge I hold against you—we will see who shall live and who shall die!"

Alice Terry uttered a terrified cry.

"Oh! no! no! you must not fight—you *must* not. It is bad—oh! so awful wicked!"

"Excuse me, lady, but you will have no voice in this matter;" and the miner's tone grew a trifle more severe. "Knew you the bitter wrong done me by this young devil with the smooth face and oily tongue— if you knew what a righteous cause I have to defend, you would say 'let the battle proceed.' I am not one to thirst for the blood of my fellow-men, but I *am* one that is ever ready to raise my hand and strike in the defense of women!"

Alice Terry secretly admired the stalwart young miner for this gallant speech.

Fearless Frank, his face paler than before, an expression of remorse combined with anguish about his countenance, and moisture standing in either eye, assumed his quasi-erect attitude as he answered:

"Edward Harris, if you will listen, I will say all I have to say in a very few words. You hate me because of a wrong I did you and yours, and you want my life for the forfeit. I shall not hinder you longer to your purpose. For two long years you have trailed and tracked me with the determination of a bloodhound, and I have evaded you, not that I was at all afraid of you, but because I did not wish to make you a murderer. I have come across your path at last; here let us settle, as you have said. See! I fold my arms across my breast. Take out your pistol, aim steadily, and fire twice at my breast. I have heard enough concerning your skill as a marksman to feel confident that you can kill me in two shots!"

Ned Harris flushed, angrily. He was surprised at the cool indifference and recklessness of the youth; he was angered that McKenzie should think *him* mean enough to take such a preposterous advantage.

"You are a fool!" he sneered, biting his lip with vexation. "Do you calculate I am a *murderer?*"

"I have no proof that you are or that you are *not!*" replied Fearless Frank, controlling his temper by a master effort. "You remember I have not kept a watch upon your actions."

"Be that as it may, I would be an accursed dog to take advantage of your insulting proposal. You must fight me the same as I shall fight you!"

"No, Ned Harris, I will do nothing of the kind. It is I who have wronged you and yours; you must take the offensive; I will play a silent hand."

"You refuse to fight me?"

"I *do* refuse to fight you, but do *not* refuse to give you satisfaction for what wrong you have suffered. Take my life, if you choose; it is yours. Take it, or forever after this consider our debt of hatred canceled, and let us be—"

"Friends? Never, Justin McKenzie, *never*! You forget the stain dyed by your hand that will never washout!"

"No! no! God knows I do not forget!" and the youth's voice was hoarse with anguish. "Could it be undone, I would gladly undo the deed. But, tell me, Harris about *her*. Does she still live?"

"*Live*? We-l-l, yes, if you can call staying living. Life is but a blank; better she had died ere she ever met you!"

"You speak truly; better she had died ere she met me."

Unconsciously the two had ridden closer to each other; had they forgotten themselves in recalling the past?

"She lives—may live on her lonely life for years to come," Harris resumed, thoughtfully, "but her life will be merely endurance."

"Will you tell me where—where I can go in secret and take but one look at her? If you will do this, I will agree to meet you and give you your chance for satis—"

"No!" thundered Harris, growing suddenly furious, "*no*! a thousand times! I'd sooner see her in the burning depths of the bottomless pit than have you get within a hundred miles of her with your contaminating presence. She is safely hidden away, and that forever, from the companionship of our sex. So let her be till death claims her!"

"You are too hard on her!"

"And not hard enough on you, base villain that your are! Who is this young lady you have to your company—another of your victims?"

"Hold! Edward Harris; enough of your vile insinuations. This lady is one whom I rescued from Sitting Bull, the Sioux, and I am helping her to hunt a father who she says is somewhere in the Black Hills. Your language should at least be respectful!"

The rebuke stung young Harris to the quick, but he reined in his passion to a moment, and doffed his hat.

"Pardon me; miss, pardon me. It was ungentlemanly for me to speak as I did, but I was surprised at seeing one of your sex in company with this accomplished scamp, Justin McKenzie."

"My presence with him is, as he said, for the purpose of finding my father. He rescued me from the Indians, and has volunteered his services, for which I am very thankful. So far, sir, he has acted in a courteous and gentlemanly manner toward me!" said Alice Terry. "What he may have been heretofore concerns me not, as you must know."

"He is always that—smooth-tongued, until he has lured his victim to ruin!" retorted Ned, bitterly. "Beware of him, lady, for he is a rattlesnake in the disguise of a bright-winged butterfly."

Fearless Frank grew livid at this last thrust. Forbearance is virtue, sometimes, but not always. In his case the Scarlet Boy felt that he could bear the taunts of the miner no longer.

"You are a liar and a dastard!" he cried, fiercely. "Come on if you wish satisfaction, and I'll give it to you!"

"I am ready, always, sir. I challenged you first; you have the choice!" retorted Ned, as cool as ever, while his enemy was all trembling with excitement.

"Pistols, at fifty yards; to be fired until one or the other is dead!" was the prompt decision.

"Good! Young lady, you will necessarily have to act as second for both of us. If I drop, leave my body where I fall, and it will be picked up by friends. If he falls, I will ride on to Deadwood, and send you out help to carry him in."

Without delay the distance was guessed at, and each of the young men rode to position. Miss Terry, the beautiful second, took her place at one side of the gulch, midway between the antagonists, and when all was to readiness she counted:

"One!"

The right hands of the two youths were raised on a level, and the gleaming barrel of a pistol shone from each.

"Two!"

There was a sharp click! click! as the hammers of the weapons were pulled back at full cock. Each click meant danger or death.

Harris was very white; so was Fearless Frank, but not so much so as the young woman who was to give the signal.

"Three! *Fire!*" cried Alice, quickly; then, there was a flash, the report of two pistols, and Ned Harris fell to the ground without a groan.

McKenzie ran to his side, and bent over him.

"Poor fellow!" he murmured, rising, a few moments later—"poor Ned. *He is dead!*"

It was Harris' request to be left where he fell. Accordingly he was laid on the grass by the roadside, his horse tethered near by, and then, accompanied by Alice, Justin McKenzie set out to Deadwood.

FOOTNOTES:

[C] Living characters

CHAPTER XI

THE POCKET GULCH MINES—INVADERS OF THEM.

We see fit to change the scene once more back to the pocket gulch—the home of the sweet, sad-faced Anita. The date is one month later—one long, eventful month since Justin McKenzie shot down Ned Harris under the noonday sun, a short distance above Deadwood.

Returning to the Flower Pocket by the route to the rugged transverse gulch, and thence through the gaping fissure, we find before us a scene—not of slumbering beauty, but of active industry and labor, such as was not here when we last looked into the flower-strewn paradise of the Hills.

The flowers are for the most part still intact, though occasionally you will come across a spot where the hand of man hath blighted their growth.

Where stood the little vine-wreathed cabin now may be seen a larger and more commodious log structure, which is but a continuation of the original.

A busy scene greets our gaze all around. Men are hurrying here and there through the valley—men not of the pale-face race, but of the red race; men, clad only to the waist, with remarkable muscular developments, and fleetness of foot.

Over the little creek which dashes far adown from pine-dressed mountain peaks, and trails its shining waters through the flowering land, is built another structure—of logs, strongly and carefully erected, and thatched by a master hand with bark and grass. From the roof projects a small smoke-stack, from which emanates a steady cloud of smoke, curling lazily upward toward heaven's blue vault, and inside is heard the grinding, crushing rumble of ponderous machinery, and we rightly conjecture that it is a crusher in full operation. Across from the northern side of the gulch comes a steady string of mules in line, each pulling behind him a jack-sled (or, what is better known to the general reader as a stone-boat) heavily laden with huge quartz rocks. These are dumped in front of one of the large doorways of the crusher, and the "empties" return mechanically and disappear within a gaping fissure in the very mountain side—a sort of tunnel, which the hand of man, aided by that great and stronger arm—powder—has burrowed and blasted out.

All this is under the immediate management of the swarthy-skinned red-men, whose faces declare them to be a remnant of the once great Ute tribe—now utilized to a better occupation than in the dark and bloody days of the past.

Near the crusher building is a large, stoutly-constructed windlass, worked by mule power, and every few moments there comes up to the surface from the depths of a shaft, a bucketful of rock and sand, which is dumped into a push-car, and from thence transferred to the line of sluice-boxes in the stream, where more half-clothed Utes are busily engaged in sifting golden particles from the rich sand.

What a transformation is all this since we left the Flower Pocket a little over a month ago! Now, everywhere within those majestic mountain-locked walls is bustle and excitement; then, the valley was sleeping away the calm, perfume-laden autumnal days, unconscious of the mines of wealth lying nestling in its bosom, and content and happy in its quietude and the adornments of nature's beauties.

Now, shouts, ringing halloos, angry curses at the obstinate mules, the rumbling of ponderous machinery, the clink of picks and reports of frequent blasts, the deadened sound of escaping steam, the barking of dogs, the whining of horses—all these sounds are now to be heard.

Then, the valley was peacefully at rest; the birds chimed in their exquisite music to the Æolian harp-like music of the breeze through the branches of the mountain pines; the waters pouring adown from the stupendous peaks created an everlasting song of love and constancy; bees and humming-birds drank delicious draughts from the blushing lips of a million nodding flowers; the sun was more hazy and drowsy-looking; everything had an appearance of ethereal peace and happiness.

But, like a drama on the stage, a grand transformation had taken place; a beautiful dream had been changed into stern reality; quietude and slumber had fled at the bold approach of bustling industry and life. And all this transformation is due to whom?

The noonday sun shone down on all the busy scene with a glance of warmth and affection, and particularly did its rays center about two men, who, standing on the southern side of the valley, up in among the rugged foothills, were watching the living panorama with the keenest interest.

They were Harry Redburn and the queer old hump-backed, bow-legged little locator, "General" Walsingham Nix.

Redburn was now looking nearly as rough, unkempt and grizzled as any veteran miner, and for a bet, he actually had not waxed the ends of his fine mustache for over a week. But there was more of a healthy glow upon his face, a robustness about his form, and a light of satisfaction in his eye which told that the rough miner's life agreed with him exceedingly well.

The old "General" was all dirt, life and animation, and as full of his eccentricities as ever. He was a character seldom met with—ever full of a quaint humor and sociability, but never known to get mad, no matter how great the provocation might be.

His chance strike upon the spot where lay the gold of Flower Pocket imbedded—if it could be called a chance, considering his dream— was the prelude to the opening up of one of the richest mining districts south of Deadwood.

We left them after Harry had driven a stake to mark the place which the somnambulist had pointed out as indicating the concealed mine.

On the succeeding day the two men set to work, and dug long and desperately to uncover the treasure, and after three days of incessant toil they were rewarded with success. A rich vein of gold, or, rather, a deposit of the valuable metal was found, it being formed in a deep, natural pocket and mixed alternately with sand and rock.

During the remaining four days of that week the two lucky miners took out enough gold to evidence their supposition that they had struck one of the richest fields in all the Black Hills country. Indeed, it seemed that there was no end to the depth of sand in the shaft, and as long as the sand held out the gold was likely to.

When, just in the flush of their early triumph, the old humpback was visited by another somnambulistic fit, and this time he discovered gold down in the northern mountain side, and prophesied that the quartz rock which could be mined therefrom would more than repay the cost and trouble of opening up the vein and of transporting machinery to the gulch.

We need not go into detail of what followed; suffice it to say that immediate arrangements were made and executed toward developing this as yet unknown territory.

While Redburn set to work with two Ute Indians (transported to the gulch from Deadwood, under oath of secrecy by the "General") to blast into the mountain-side, and get at the gold-bearing quartz, the old locater in person set out for Cheyenne on the secret mission of procuring a portable crusher, boiler and engine, and such other implements as would be needed, and getting them safely into the gulch unknown to the roving population of the Hills country. And most wonderful to relate, he succeeded.

Two weeks after his departure, he returned with the machinery and two score of Ute Indians, whom he had sworn into his service, for, as a Ute rarely breaks his word, they were likely to prove valuable accessories to the plans of our two friends. Redburn had in the meantime blasted in until he came upon the quartz rock. Here he had to stop until the arrival of the machinery. He however busied himself in enlarging the cabin and building a curb to the shaft, which occupied his time until at last the "General" and his army returned.[D]

Now, we see these two successful men standing and gazing at the result of their joint labors, each financially happy; each growing rich as the day rolls away.

The miners are in a prosperous condition, and everything moves off with that ease and order that speaks of shrewd management and constant attention to business.

The gold taken from the shaft is much finer than that extracted from the quartz.

The quartz yielded about eighteen dollars to the ton, which the "General" declared to be as well as "a feller c'u'd expect, considerin' things, more or less!"

Therefore, it will be seen by those who have any knowledge whatever of gold mining that, after paying off the expenses, our friends were not doing so badly, after all.

"Yes, yes!" the "General" was remarking, as he gazed at the string of mules that alternately issued from and re-entered the fissure on the opposite side of the valley; "yes, yes, boyee, things ar' workin' as I like ter see 'em at last. The shaft'll more'n pay expenses if she holds her head 'bove water, as I opine she will, an' w'at ar' squeezed out uv the quartz ar' cleer 'intment fer us."

"True; the shaft is more than paying off the hands," replied Redburn, seating himself upon a bowlder, and staring vacantly at the dense column of smoke ejected from the smoke-stack in the roof of the crusher building.

"I was looking up accounts last evening, and after deducting what you paid for the machinery, and what wages are due the Utes, we have about a thousand dollars clear of all, to be divided between three of us."

"Exactly. Now, that's w'at I call fair to middling. Of course thar'll be more or less expense, heerafter, but et'll be a consider'ble less o' more than more o' less. Another munth'll tell a larger finanshell tale, I opine"

"Right again, unless something happens more than we think for now. If we get through another month, however, without being nosed out, why we may consider ourselves all-fired lucky."

"Jes' so! Jes' so! but we'll hev ter take our chances. One natteral advantage, we kin shute 'em as fast as they come—"

"Ho!" Redburn interrupted, suddenly, leaping to his feet; "they say the devil's couriers are ever around when you are talking of them. Look! invaders already."

He pointed toward the east, where the passage led out of the valley into the gorge beyond.

Out of this passage two persons on horseback had just issued, and now they came to a halt, evidently surprised at the scene which lay spread out before them.

No sooner did the "General" clap his eyes on the pair than he uttered a cry of astonishment, mingled with joy.

"It's thet scarlet chap, Fearless Frank!" he announced, hopping about like a pig on a hot griddle "w'at I war tellin' ye about; the same cuss w'at desarted Charity Joe's train, ter look fer sum critter w'at war screechin' fer help. I went wi' the lad fer a ways, but my jackass harpened to be more or less indispositioned—consider'bly more o' less than less o' more—an' so I made up my mind not ter continny his route. Ther last I see'd o' the lad he disappeared over sum kind o' a precypice, an' calkylatin' as how he war done fer, I rej'ined Charity Joseph, ar' kim on."

"He has a female in his company!" said Redburn, watching the new-comer keenly.

"Yas, peers to me he has, an' et's more or less likely that et's the same critter he went to resky w'en he left Charity Joe's train!"

"What about him? We do not want him here; to let him return to Deadwood after what he has seen would be certain death to our interests."

"Yas, thar's more or less truth in them words o' yours, b'yee— consider'bly more o' less than less o' more. He ken't go back now, nohow we kin fix et. He's a right peart sort o' a kid, an' I think ef we was ter guv him a job, or talk reeson'ble ter him, thet he'd consent to do the squar' thing by us."

Redburn frowned.

"He'll have to remain for a certain time, whether he wants to or not," he muttered, more savage than usual. It looked to him as if this was to be the signal of a general invasion. "Come! let's go and see what we can do."

They left the foothills, clambered down into the valley and worked their way toward where Fearless Frank and his companion sat in waiting.

As they did so, headed by a figure in black, who wore a mask as did all the rest, a band of horsemen rode out of the fissure into the valley. One glance and we recognize Deadwood Dick, Prince of the Road, and his band of road-agents!

CHAPTER XII

MAKING TERMS ALL AROUND.

Old General Nix was the first to discover the new invasion.

"Gorra'mighty!" he ejaculated, flourishing his staff about excitedly, "d'je mind them same w'at's tuk et inter the'r heads to invade our sancty sanctorum, up yander? Howly saints frum ther cullender! We shall be built up inter an entire city 'twixt this an' sunset, ef ther population n' sect becum enny more numersome. Thars a full fifty o' them sharks, more or less—consider'bly more o' less than less o' more—an' ef we hain't got ter hold a full hand in order ta clean 'em out, why, ye can call me a cross-eyed, hair lipped hyeeny, that's all."

Redburn uttered an ejaculation as he saw the swarm of invaders that was perhaps more forcible than polite.

He did not like the looks of things at all. If Ned Harris were only here, he thought, he could throw the responsibility all off on his shoulders. But he was not; neither had he been seen or heard of since he had quitted the valley over a month ago. Where he was staying all this time was a problem that no one could solve—no one among our three friends.

The "General" had made inquiries in Deadwood, but elicited no information concerning the young miner. He had dropped entirely out of the magic city's notice, and might be dead or dying in some foreign clime, for all they knew. Anita worried and grew sadder each day at his non-return; it seemed to her that he was in distress, or worse, perhaps—dead. He had never stayed away so long before, she said, always returning from his trips every few days. What, then, could now be the reason of his prolonged absence?

Redburn foresaw trouble in the intrusion of the road-agents and Fearless Frank, although he knew not the character or calling of the former, and he resolved to make one bold stroke in defense of the mines.

"Go to the quartz mines as quickly as you can!" he said, addressing Nix, "and call every man to his arms. Then rally them out here, where I will be waiting with the remainder of our forces, and we will see what can be done. If it is to be a fight for our rights, a desperate fight it shall be."

The "General" hurried off with as much alacrity as was possible, with him, toward the quartz mine, while Redburn likewise made haste to visit the shaft and collect together his handful of men.

He passed the cabin on the way, and, seeing Anita seated in the doorway, he came to a momentary halt.

"You had better go inside and lock the doors and windows behind you," he said, advisingly. "There are invaders in the gulch, and we must try and effect a settlement with them; so it is not desirable that they should see you."

"You are not going to fight them?"

"Yes, if they will not come to reasonable terms which I shall name. Why?"

"Oh! don't fight. You will get killed."

"Humph! what of that? Who would care if I were killed?"

"I would, for one, Mr. Redburn."

The miner's heart gave a great bound, and he gazed into the pure white face of the girl, passionately. Was it possible that she had in her heart anything akin to love, for *him*? Already be had conceived a passing fancy for her, which might ripen into love, in time.

"Thanks!" he said, catching up her hand and pressing it to his lips. "Those words, few as they are, make me happy, Miss Anita. But, stop! I must away. Go inside, and keep shady until you see me again;" and so saying he hurried on.

In ten minutes' time two score of brawny, half-dressed Utes were rallied in the valley, and Redburn was at their head, accompanied by the "General."

"I will now go forward and hold parley," said Harry, as he wrapped a kerchief about the muzzle of his rifle-barrel. "If you see me fall, you can calculate that it's about time for you to sling in a chunk of your lip."

He had fallen into the habit of talking in an illiterate fashion, since his association with the "General."

"All right," assented the old locater; "ef they try ter salt ye, jes' giv' a squawk, an' we'll cum a-tearin' down ter yer resky at ther rate o' forty hours a mile, more or less—consider'bly more o' less than less o' more."

Redburn buckled his belt a hole tighter, looked to his two revolvers, and set out on his mission.

The road-agents had, in the mean time, circled off to the right of the fissure, and formed into a compact body, where they halted and watched the rallying of the savages in the valley.

Fearless Frank and his lovely companion remained where they had first halted, awaiting developments. They had stumbled into Paradise and were both surprised and bewildered.

Redburn approached them first. He was at loss how to open the confab, but the Scarlet Boy saved him the trouble.

"I presume I see in you one of the representatives of this concern," he said, doffing his hat and showing his pearly teeth in a little smile, as the miner came up.

"You do," replied Redburn, bowing stiffly. "I am an owner or partner in this mining enterprise, which, until your sudden advent, has been a secret to the outside world."

"I believe you, pilgrim; for, though I am pretty thoroughly acquainted with the topography of the Black Hills country, I had not the least idea that such an enterprise existed in this part of the territory."

"No, I dare say not. But how is it that we are indebted to you for this intrusion?—for such we feel justified in calling it, under the existing circumstances."

"I did not intend to intrude, sir, nor do I now. In riding through the mountains we accidentally stumbled into the fissure passage that leads to this gulch, and as there was nothing to hinder us, we came on through."

"True; I should have posted a strong guard in the pass. You have a female companion, I perceive; not your wife?"

"Oh, no! nor my sister, either. This is Miss Terry—an estimable young lady, who has come to the Black Hills in search of her father. Your name is—"

"Redburn—Harry Redburn; and yours, I am told, is Fearless Frank."

"Yes, that is the title I sail under. But how do you know aught of me?"

"I was told your name by a partner of mine. Now, then, concerning the present matter; what do you propose to do?"

"To do? Why, turn back, I suppose; I see nothing else to do."

Redburn leaned on his rifle and considered.

"Do you belong to that other crowd?"

"No, indeed;" Frank's face flushed, half angrily. "I thank my stars I am not quite so low down as that, yet. Do you know them? That's Deadwood Dick, the Prince of the Road, and his band of outlaws!"

"What—is it possible? The same gang whom the *Pioneer* is making such a splurge over, every week."

"The same. That fellow clad in black is Deadwood Dick, the leader."

"Humph! He in black; you in scarlet. Two contrasting colors."

"That is so. I had not thought of it before. But no significance is attached thereto."

"Perhaps not. Have you the least idea what brought them here?"

"The road-agents? I reckon I do. The military has been chasing them for the last two days. Probably they have come here for protection."

"Maybe so; or for plunder. Give me your decision, and I will go and see what they want."

"There is nothing for me to decide more than to take the back track."

Redburn shook his head, decidedly.

"You cannot go back!" he said, using positiveness in his argument; "that is, not for awhile. You'd have all Deadwood down on us in a jiffy. I'll give you work in the shaft, at three dollars a day. You can accept that offer, or submit to confinement until I see fit to set you at liberty."

"And my companion, here—?"

"I will place under the charge of Miss Anita for the present, where she will receive hospitable treatment."

Fearless Frank started as though he had been struck a violent blow; his face grew very white; his eyes dilated; he trembled in every joint.

"*Anita!*" he gasped—"*Anita!*"

"I believe that is what I said!" Redburn could not understand the youth's agitation. He knew that the sister of Ned Harris had a secret; was this Fearless Frank in any way connected with it, and if so, how? "Do you know her?"

"Her other name is—"

"Harris—Anita Harris, in full. Do you know her, or aught of her?"

"I—I—I did, once!" was the slow reply. "Where is she; I want to see her?"

Redburn took a moment to consider.

Would it be best to permit a meeting between the two until he should be able to learn something more definite concerning the secret? If Ned Harris were here would he sanction such a meeting? No! something told the young miner that he would not; something warned him that it could result in no good to allow the scarlet youth an interview with sad, sweet-faced Anita.

"You cannot see her!" he at last said, decidedly. "There is a reason why you two should never meet again, and if you remain in the gulch, as you will be obliged to, for the present, you must give me your word of honor that you will not go near yonder cabin."

Fearless Frank had expected this; therefore he was not surprised. Neither did Redburn know how close he had shied his stone at the real truth.

"I promise," McKenzie said, after a moment's deliberation, "on my honor, that I will not approach the cabin, providing you will furnish me my meals and lodgings elsewhere. If Anita comes to me, what then?"

"I will see that she does not," Redburn answered, positively. Gradually he was assuming full control of things, in the absence of Harris, himself. "Miss Terry, you may ride down to yonder cabin, and tell Anita I sent you. Pilgrim, you can come along with me."

"No; I will accompany Alice as far as where your forces are stationed," said Frank, and then they rode down the slope, Redburn turning toward where the road-agents sat upon their horses in a compact body, with Deadwood Dick at their head.

As the miner drew nigh and came to a standstill, the Prince of the road rode forward to his side.

"Well—?" he said, interrogatively, his voice heavy yet pleasant; "I suppose you desire to know what bizness we've got in your cornfield, eh, stranger?"

"That's about the dimensions of it, yes," replied Redburn, at once conceiving a liking for the young road-agent, in whom he thought he saw a true gentleman, in the disguise of a devil. "I came over to learn the object you have in view, in invading our little valley, if you have no objections in telling."

"Certainly not. As you may have guessed already, we are a band of road-agents, whose field of action we have lately confined to the Black Hills country. I have the honor of being the leader, and you have doubtless heard of me—Deadwood Dick, the 'Road-Agent Prince,' as the *Pioneer* persists in terming me. Just at present, things are rather sultry in the immediate vicinity of Deadwood, so far as we are concerned, and we sought this locality to escape a small army of the Deadwood military, who have been nosing around after us for the past week."

"Well—?"

"Well, we happened to see a man and woman come this way, and believing that it must lead to somewhere or other, we followed, and here we are, out of the reach of the blue-coats, but, I take it, *in* the way of a party of secret miners. Is it not so?"

"No, not necessarily so, unless you put yourselves in the way. You wish to remain quartered here for the present?"

"If not contrary to your wishes, we should like to, yes."

"I have no objections to offer, providing you will agree to two points."

"And what are they, may I ask?"

"These. That you will camp at the mouth of the passage, and thus keep out any other intruders that may come; second, that you will keep your men to this side or the valley, and not interfere with any of our laborers."

"To which I eagerly agree. You shall experience no inconvenience from our presence here; you furnish us a haven of safety from the pursuing soldiers; we in return will extend you our aid in repelling a host of fortune-seekers who may any moment come down this way in swarms."

"Very well; that settles it, then. You keep your promise, and all will go well."

The two shook hands: then Redburn turned and strode back to dismiss his forces, while Dick and his men took up their position at the place where the fissure opened into the gulch. Here they made preparations to camp. Redburn, while returning to his men, heard a shout of joy, and looking up, saw, to his surprise, that the old "General" and Alice Terry were locked in each other's arms, in a loving embrace.

FOOTNOTES:

[D] This crusher is said to have been the first introduced into the Black Hills

CHAPTER XIII.

AT THE CABIN.

What did it mean?

Had the old hump-backed, bow-legged mine-locater gone crazy, or was he purposely insulting the beautiful maiden? Fearless Frank stood aside, apparently offering no objections to the hugging, and the Indians did likewise.

At least Miss Terry made no serious attempts to free herself from the "General's" bear-like embrace.

A few bounds brought Redburn to the spot, panting, breathless, perspiring. "What is the meaning of this disgraceful scene?" he demanded, angrily.

"Disgraceful!" The old "General" set Miss Terry down on her feet, after giving her a resounding smack, and turned to stare at the young miner, in astonishment. "Disgraceful! Waal, young man, ter tell the solid Old Testament truth, more or less—consider'bly less o' more 'n more o' less—I admire yer cheek, hard an' unblushin' as et ar'. Ye call my givin' this pretty piece o' feminine gander a squar', fatherly sort o' a hug, *disgraceful*, do ye? Think et's all out o' ther bounds o' propriety, do ye?"

"I look at it in that light, yes," Redburn replied.

"Haw! haw! haw!" and the General shook his fat sides with immoderate laughter. "Why, pilgrim-tender-fut, this 'ere hundred an' twenty-six pounds o' feminine gender b'longs to me—ter yours, truly, Walsingham Nix—an' I have a parfec' indervidual right ter hug an' kiss her as much as I please, wi'out brookin' enny interference frum you. Alice, dear, this ar' Harry Redburn, ginerall sup'intendent o' ther Flower Pocket gold-mines, an' 'bout as fair specimen as they make, nowadays. Mr. Redburn, I'll formally present you to Miss Alice Terry, *my darter!*"

Redburn colored, and was not a little disconcerted on account of his blunder; but he rallied in a moment, and acknowledged the introduction with becoming grace and dignity.

"You must excuse my interference," he said, earnestly. "I saw the old 'General' here taking liberties that no stranger should take, and knowing nothing of the relationship existing between you, I was naturally inclined to think that he was either drunk or crazy; therefore I deemed it necessary to investigate. No offense, I hope."

"Of course not." and Alice smiled one of her sweetest smiles. "You did perfectly right and are deserving of no censure, whatever."

After a few moments of desultory conversation, Redburn took the "General" to one side, and spoke on the subject of Fearless Frank and Anita Harris—of his action in the matter, and so forth. Nix—or Terry, as the latter was evidently his real name—heartily coincided with his views, and both agreed that it was best not to let the Scarlet Boy come within range of Anita, or, at least, not till Ned Harris should return, when he could do as he chose.

Accordingly it was decided that Fearless Frank should be set to work in the quartz mine, that being the furthest from the cabin, and he could eat and sleep either in the mine or in the crusher building, whichever he liked best.

After settling this point the two men rejoined the others, and Frank was apprised of their decision. He made no remarks upon it, but it was plain to see that he was anything but satisfied. His wild spirit yearned for constant freedom.

The Utes were dismissed and sent back to their work; the "General" strolled off with McKenzie toward the quartz mine; it devolved upon Redburn to escort Alice to the cabin, which he did with pleasure, and gave her an introduction to sweet, sad-faced Anita, who awaited their coming in the open doorway.

The two girls greeted each other with warmth; it was apparent that they would become fast friends when they learned more of each other.

As for Redburn, he was secretly enamored with the "General's" pretty daughter; she was beautiful, and evidently accomplished, and her progenitor was financially well-to-do. What then was lacking to make her a fitting mate for any man? Redburn pondered deeply on this subject, as he left the girls together, and went out to see to his duties in the mines.

He found Terry and Fearless Frank in the quartz mine, looking at the swarthy-skinned miners; examining new projected slopes; suggesting easier methods for working out different lumps of gold-bearing rock. While the former's knowledge of practical mining was extended, the latter's was limited.

"I think thet thar ar' bigger prospects yet, in further," the old locater was saying. "I ain't much varsed on jeeological an' toppygraffical formation, myself, ye see; but then, it kinder 'peers to me thet this quartz vein ar' a-goin' to hold out fer a consider'ble time yet."

"Doubtless. More straight digging an' less slopes I should think would be practicable," McKenzie observed.

"I don't see it!" said Redburn, joining them. "Sloping and transversing discovers new veins, while line work soon plays out. I think things are working in excellent order at present."

They all made a tour of the mine which had been dug a considerable distance into the mountain. The quartz was ordinarily productive, and being rather loosely thrown together was blasted down without any extra trouble. After a short consultation, Redburn and the "General" concluded to place Frank over the Utes as superintendent and mine-boss, as they saw that he was not used to digging, blasting or any of the rough work connected with the mine, although he was clear-headed and inventive.

When tendered the position it was gratefully accepted by him, he expressing it his intention to work for the interest of his employers as long as he should stay in the gulch.

Night at last fell over the Flower Pocket gold-mines, and work ceased.

The Utes procured their own food—mainly consisting of fish from the little creek and deer and mountain birds that could be brought down at almost any hour from the neighboring crags—and slept in the open air. Redburn had McKenzie a comfortable bed made in the crusher-house, and sent him out a meal fit for a prince.

As yet, Anita knew nothing of the scarlet youth's identity;—scarcely knew, in fact, that he was in the valley.

At the cabin, the evening meal was dispatched with a general expression of cheerfulness about the board. Anita seemed less downcast than usual, and the vivacious Alice made life and merriment for all. She was witty where wit was proper, and sensible in an unusual degree.

Redburn was infatuated with her. He watched her with an expression of fondness in his eyes; he admired her every gesture and action; he saw something new to admire in her, each moment he was in her society.

When the evening meal was cleared away, he took down the guitar, and sung several ballads, the old "General" accompanying him with his rich deep bass, and Alice with her clear birdlike alto; and the sweet melody of the trio's voices called forth round after round of rapturous applause from the road-agents camped upon the slope, and from the Utes who were lounging here and there among the flower-beds of the valley. But of the lot, Deadwood Dick was the only one bold enough to approach the cabin, he came sauntering along and halted on the threshold, nodding to the occupants of the little apartment with a nonchalance which was not assumed.

"Good-evening!" he said, tipping his sombrero, but taking care not to let the mask slip from his face. "I hope mine is not an intrusion. Hearing music, I was loth to stay away, for I am a great lover of music;—it is the one passion that appeals to my better nature."

He seated himself on the little stone step, and motioned for Redburn to proceed.

One of those inside the cabin had been strangely affected at the sight of Dick, and that person was Anita. She turned deathly pale, her eyes assumed an expression of affright, and she trembled violently, as she first saw him. The Prince of the Road, however, if he saw her, noticed not her agitation; in fact, he took not the second glance at her while he remained at the cabin. His eyes were almost constantly fastening upon the lovely face and form of Alice.

Thinking it best to humor one who might become either a powerful enemy or an influential friend, Redburn accordingly struck up a lively air, *a la banjo,* and in exact imitation of a minstrel, rendered "Gwine to Get a Home, Bymeby." And the thunders of *encore* that came from the outside listeners, showed how surely he had touched upon a pleasant chord. He followed that with several modern serio-comic songs, all of which were received well and heartily applauded.

"That recalls memories of good old times," said the road-agent, as he leaned back against the door-sill, and gazed at the mountains, grand, majestic, stupendous, and the starlit sky, azure, calm and serene. "Recalls the days of early boyhood, that were gay, pure, and happy. Ah! ho!"

He heaved a deep sign, and his head dropped upon his breast.

A deathlike silence pervaded the cabin; that one heartfelt sigh aroused a sensation of pity in each of the four hearts that beat within the cabin walls.

That the road-agent was a gentleman in disguise, was not to be gainsayed; all felt that, despite his outlawed calling, he was deserving of a place among them, in his better moods.

As if to accord with his mood, Alice began a sweet birdlike song, full of tender pathos, and of quieting sympathy.

It was a quaint Scottish melody,—rich in its honeyed meaning, sweetly weird and pitiful; wonderfully soothing and nourishing to a weeping spirit.

Clear and flute-like the maiden's cultured voice swelled out on the still night air, and the mountain echoes caught up the strains and lent a wild peculiar accompaniment.

Deadwood Dick listened, with his head still bowed, and his hands clasped about one knee;—listened in a kind of fascination, until the last reverberations of the song had died out in a wailing echo; then he sprung abruptly to his feet, drew one hand wearily across the masked brow; raised his sombrero with a deft movement, and bowed himself out—out into the night, where the moon and stars looked down at him, perhaps with more lenience than on some.

Alice Terry rose from her seat, crossed over to the door, and gazed after the straight handsome form, until it had mingled with the other road-agents, who had camped upon the slope. Then she turned about, and sat down on the couch beside Anita.

"You are still, dear," she said, stroking the other's long, unconfined hair. "Are you lonely? If not why don't you say something?"

"I have nothing to say," replied Anita, a sad, sweet smile playing over her features. "I have been too much taken up with the music to think of talking."

"But, you are seldom talkative."

"So brother used to tell me. He said I had lost my heart, and tongue."

Redburn was drumming on the window-casing with his fingers;—a sort of lonely tattoo it was.

"You seemed to be much interested in the outlaw. Miss Terry," he observed, as if by chance the thought had just occurred to him, when, in reality, he was downright jealous. "Had you two ever met—"

"Certainly not, sir," and Alice flashed him an inquiring glance. "Why do you ask?"

"Oh! for no reason, in particular, only I fancied that song was meant especially for him."

Redburn, afterward, would have given a hundred dollars to have recalled those words, for the haughty, half-indignant look Alice gave him instantly showed him he was on the wrong track.

If he wished to court her favor, it must be in a different way, and he must not again give her a glimpse of his jealous nature.

"You spoke of a brother," said Alice, turning to Anita. "Does he live here with you?"

"Yes, when not away on business. He has now been absent for over a month."

"Indeed! Is he as sweet, sad, and silent as yourself?"

"Oh! no; Ned is unlike me; he is buoyant, cheerful, pleasant."

"Ned? What is his full name, dear?"

"Edward Harris."

Alice grew suddenly pale and speechless, as she remembered the handsome young miner whom Fearless Frank had slain in the duel, just outside of Deadwood. This, then, was his sister; and evidently she as yet knew nothing of his sad fate.

"Do you know aught concerning Edward Harris?" Redburn asked, seeing her agitation. Alice considered a moment.

"I do," she answered, at last. "This Fearless Frank, whom I came here with, had a duel with a man, just above Deadwood, whose name was Edward Harris!"

"My God;—and his fate—?"

"He was instantly killed, and left lying where he dropped!"

There was a scream of agony, just here, and a heavy fall.

Anita had fainted!

CHAPTER XIV.

THE TRANSIENT TRIUMPH.

Redburn sprung from his seat, ran over to her side, and raised her tenderly in his arms.

"Poor thing!" he murmured, gazing into her pale, still face, "the shock was too much for her. No wonder she fainted." He laid her on the couch, and kept off the others who crowded around.

"Bring cold water!" he ordered, "and I will soon have her out of this fit."

Alice hastened to obey, and Anita's face and hands were bathed in the cooling liquid until she began to show signs of returning consciousness.

"You may now give me the particulars of the affair," Redburn said, rising and closing the door, for a chilly breeze was sweeping into the cabin.

Alice proceeded to comply with his request by narrating what had occurred and, as nearly as possible, what had been said. When she had concluded, he gazed down for several moments thoughtfully into the face of Anita. There was much yet that was beyond his powers of comprehension—a knotty problem for which he saw no immediate solution.

"What do you think about it, "General"?" he asked, turning to the mine-locater. "Have we sufficient evidence to hang this devil in scarlet?"

"Hardly, boyee, hardly. 'Peers te me, 'cordin' to ther gal's tell, thet thar war a fair shake all around, an' as duelin' ar' more or less ther fashun 'round these parts,—considera'bly more o' less 'n less o' more—et ain't law-fell ter yank a critter up by ther throat!"

"I know it is not, according to the customs of this country of the Black Hills; but, look at it. That fellow, who I am satisfied is a black-hearted knave, has not only taken the life of poor Harris, but, very probably, has given his sister her death-blow. The question is: should he go unpunished in the face of all this evidence?"

"Yes. Let him go; *I* will be the one to punish him!"

It was Anita who spoke. She had partly arisen on the couch; her face was streaked with water and slightly haggard; her hair blew unconfined about her neck and shoulders; her eyes blazed with a wild, almost savage fire.

"Let him go!" she repeated, more of fierceness in her voice than Redburn had ever heard there, before. "He shall not escape my vengeance. Oh, my poor, poor dead brother!"

She flung herself back upon the couch, and gave herself up to a wild, passionate, uncontrollable outburst of tears and sobs—the wailings of a sorrowing heart. For a long time she continued to weep and sob violently; then came a lull, during which she fell asleep, from exhaustion—a deep sleep. Redburn and Alice then carried her into an adjoining room, where she was left under the latter's skillful care. Awhile later the cabin was wrapped in silence.

When morning sunlight next peeped down into the Flower Pocket, it found everything generally astir. Anita was up and pursuing her household duties, but she was calm, now, even sadder than before, making a strange contrast to blithe, gaysome Alice, who flitted about, here and there, like some bright-winged butterfly surrounded by a halo of perpetual sunshine.

Unknown to any one save themselves, two men were within the valley of the Flower Pocket gold-mines—there on business, and that business meant bloodshed. They were secreted in among the foothills on the western side of the flowering paradise, at a point where they were not observed, and at the same time were the observers of all that was going on in front of them.

How came they here, when the hand of Deadwood Dick guarded the only accessible entrance there was to the valley? The answer was:

they came secretly through the pass on the night preceding the arrival of the road-agents, and had been lying in close concealment ever since.

The one was an elderly man of portly figure, and the other a young, dandyish fellow, evidently the elder's son, for they resembled each other in every feature. We make no difficulty to recognizing them as the same precious pair whom Outlaw Dick captured from the stage, only to lose them again through the treachery of two of his own band.

Both looked considerably the worse for wear, and the gaunt, hungry expression on their features, as the morning sunlight shone down upon them, declared in a language more adequate than words, that they were beginning to suffer the first pangs of starvation.

"We cannot hold out at this rate much longer!" the elder Filmore cried, as he watched the bustle in the valley below. "I'm as empty as a collapsed balloon, and what's more, we're in no prospects of immediate relief."

Filmore, the younger, groaned aloud in agony of spirit.

"Curse the Black Hills and all who have been fools enough to inhabit them, anyhow!" he growled, savagely; "just let me get back in the land of civilization again, and you can bet your bottom dollar I'll know enough to stay there."

"Bah! this little rough experience will do you good. If we only had a square meal or two and a basket of sherry, I should feel quite at home. Nothing but a fair prospect of increasing our individual finances would ever have lured me into this outlandish place. But money, you know, is the root of all—"

"Evil!" broke in the other, "and after three months' wild-goose-chase you are just as destitute of the desired root as you were at first."

"True, but we have at least discovered one of the shrubs at the bottom of which grows the root."

"You refer to Deadwood Dick?"

"I do. He is here in the valley, and he must never leave it alive. While we have the chance we must strike the blow that will forever silence his tongue."

"Yes; but what about the girl? She will be just as much in the way, if not a good deal more so."

"We can manage her all right when the proper time arrives. Dick is our game, now."

"He may prove altogether too much game. But, now that we are counting eggs, how much of the 'lay' is to be mine, when this boy and girl are finished?" he queried.

"How much? Well, that depends upon circumstances. The girl *may* fall to you."

"The girl? Bah! I'd rather be excused."

The day passed without incident in the mines. The work went steadily on, the sounds of the crusher making strange music for the mountain echoes to mock.

Occasionally the crack of a rifle announced that either a road-agent or a Ute miner had risked a shot at a mountain sheep, bird, or deer. Generally their aim was attended with success, though sometimes they were unable to procure the slaughtered game.

Redburn, on account of his clear-headedness and business tact, had full charge of both mines, the "General" working under him in the shaft, and Fearless Frank in the quartz mine.

When questioned about his duel with Harris by Redburn, McKenzie had very little to say; he seemed pained when approached on the subject; would answer no questions concerning the past; was reserved and at times singularly haughty.

During the day Anita and Alice took a stroll through the valley, but the latter had been warned, and fought shy of the quartz mine; so there was no encounter between Anita and Fearless Frank.

Deadwood Dick joined them as they were returning to the cabin, loaded down with flowers—flowers of almost every color and perfume.

"This is a beautiful day," he remarked, pulling up a daisy, as he walked gracefully along. "One rarely sees so many beauties centered in one little valley like this—beautiful landscape and mountain scenery, beautiful flowers beneath smiling skies, and lovely women, the chief center of attraction among all."

"Indeed!" and Alice gave him a coquettish smile; "you are flattering, sir road-agent. You, at least, are not beautiful, in that horrible black suit and villainous mask. You remind me of a picture I have seen somewhere of the devil in disguise; all that is lacking is the horns, tail and cloven-foot."

Dick broke out into a burst of laughter—it was one of those wild, terrible laughs of his, so peculiar to hear from one who was evidently young in years.

Both of the girls were terrified, and would have fled had he not detained them.

"Ha, ha!" he said, stepping in front of them, "do not be frightened; don't go, ladies. That's only the way I express my amusement at anything."

"Then, for mercy's sake, don't get amused again," said Alice, deprecatingly. "Why, dear me, I thought the Old Nick and all his couriers had pounced down upon us."

"Well, how do you know but what he has? *I* may be his Satanic majesty, or one of his envoys."

"I hardly think so; you are too much an earthly being for that. Come, now, take off that detestable mask and let me see what you look like."

"No, indeed! I would not remove this mask, except on conditions, for all the gold yon toiling miners are finding, which, I am satisfied, is no small amount."

"You spoke of conditions. What are they?"

"Some time, perhaps, I will tell you, lady, but not now. See! my men are signaling to me, and I must go. Adieu, ladies;" and in another moment he had wheeled, and was striding back toward camp.

In their concealment the two Filmores witnessed this meeting between Dick and the two girls.

"So there are females here, eh?" grunted the elder, musingly. "From observation I should say that Prince Dick was a comparative stranger here."

"That is my opinion," groaned Clarence, his thoughts reverting to his empty stomach. "Did you hear that laugh a moment ago? It was more like the screech of a lunatic than anything else."

"Yes; he is a young tiger. There is no doubt of that to my mind."

"And we shall have to keep on the alert to take him. He came to the cabin last night. If he does to-night we can mount him!"

Before night the elder Filmore succeeded in capturing a wild goose that had strayed down with the stream from somewhere above. This was killed, dressed and half cooked by a brushwood fire which they hazarded in a fissure in the hillside whereto they had hidden. This fowl they almost ravenously devoured, and thus thoroughly satisfied their appetites. They now felt a great deal better, ready for the work in hand—of capturing and slaying the dare-devil Deadwood Dick.

As soon as it was dark they crept, like the prowling wolves they were, down into the valley, and positioned themselves midway between the cabin and the road-agent's camp, but several yards apart, with a lasso held above the grass between them, to serve as a "trip-up."

The sky had become overcast with dense black clouds, and the gloom to the valley was quite impenetrable. From their concealment the two Filmores could hear Redburn, Alice and the "General" singing up at the cabin, and it told them to be on their guard, as Dick might now come along at any moment.

Slowly the minutes dragged by, and both were growing impatient, when the firm tread of "the Prince" was heard swiftly approaching.

Quickly the lasso was drawn taut. Dick, not dreaming of the trap, came boldly along, tripped, and went sprawling to the ground. The next instant his enemies were on him, each with a long murderous knife in hand.

CHAPTER XV.

TO THE RESCUE!

The suddenness of the onslaught prevented Deadwood Dick from raising a hand to defend himself, and the two strong men piling their combined weights upon him, had the effect to render him utterly helpless. He would have yelled to apprise his comrades of his fate, but Alexander Filmore, ready for the emergency, quickly thrust a cob of wood into his mouth, and bound it there with strong strings.

The young road-agent was a prisoner.

"Hal ha!" leered the elder Filmore, peering down into the masked face—"ha! ha! my young eaglet; so I have you at last, have I? After repeated efforts to get you in my power, I have at last been rewarded with success, eh? Ha! ha! the terrible scourge of the Black Hills lies here at my feet, mine to do with as I shall see fit."

"Shall we settle him, and leave him lying here, where his gang can find him?" interrupted the younger Filmore, who, now that his blood was up, cared little what he did. "You give him one jab, and I will guarantee to finish him with the second!"

"No! no! boy; you are too hasty. Before we silence him, forever, we must ascertain, if possible, where the girl is."

"But, he'll never tell us."

"We have that yet to find out. It is my opinion that we can bring him to terms, somehow. Take hold, and we will carry him back to our hole in the hill."

Deadwood Dick was accordingly seized by the neck and heels, and borne swiftly and silently toward the western side of the gulch, up among the foothills, into the rift, where the plotters had lain concealed since their arrival. Here he was placed upon the ground in a sitting posture, and his two enemies crouched on either side of him, like beasts ready to spring upon their prey.

Below in the valley, the Utes had kindled one solitary fire, and this with a starlike gleam of light from the cabin window, was the only sign of life to be seen through the night's black shroud. The trio in the foothills were evidently quite alone.

Alexander Filmore broke the silence.

"Well, my gay Deadwood Dick, Prince of the Road, I suppose you wish to have the matter over with, as soon as possible"

The road-agent nodded.

"Better let him loose in the jaws," suggested Filmore the younger; "or how else shall we get from him what we must know? Take out his gag. I'll hold my six against his pulsometer. If he squawks, I'll silence him, sure as there is virtue in powder and ball!"

The elder, after some deliberation, acquiesced, and Dick was placed in possession of his speaking power, while the muzzle of young Filmore's revolver pressed against his breast, warned him to silence and obedience.

"Now," said the elder Filmore, "just you keep mum. If you try any trickery, it will only hasten your destruction, which is inevitable!"

Deadwood Dick gave a little laugh.

"You talk as if you were going to do something toward making me the center of funeralistic attraction."

"You'll find out, soon enough, young man. I have not pursued you so long, all for nothing, you may rest assured. Your death will be the only event that can atone for all the trouble you have given me, in the past."

"*Is* that so? Well, you seem to hold all the *trump* cards, and I reckon you ought to win, though I can't see into your inordinate thirst for *diamonds*, when *spades* will eventually triumph. Had I a *full hand* of *clubs*, I am not so sure but what I could *raise* you, *knaves* though you are!"

"I think not; when kings win, the game is virtually up. We hold altogether to high cards for you, at present, and *beg* as you may, we shall not *pass* you."

"Don't be too sure of it. The best trout often slips from the hook, when you are sanguine that you have at last been immoderately successful. But, enough of this cheap talk. Go on and say your say, in as few words as possible, for I am in a hurry."

Both Filmore, Sr., and Filmore, Jr., laughed at this—it sounded so ridiculously funny to hear a helpless prisoner talk of being in a hurry.

"Business must be pressing!" leered the elder, savagely. "Don't be at all scared. We'll start you humming along the road to Jordan soon enough, if that's what you want. First, however, we desire you to inform us where we can find the girl, as we wish to make a clean sweep, while we are about it."

"Do you bathe your face in alum-water?" abruptly asked the road-agent, staring at his captor, quizzically. "Do you?"

"Bathe in *alum*-water? Certainly not, sir. Why do you ask?"

"Because the hardness of you cheek is highly suggestive of the use of some similar application."

Alexander Filmore stared at his son a moment, at loss to comprehend; but, as it began to dawn upon him that he was the butt of a hard hit, he uttered a frightful curse.

"My cheek and your character bear a close resemblance, then!" he retorted, hotly. "Again I ask you, will you tell me where the girl is?"

"No! you must take me for an ornery mule, or some other kind of an animal, if you think I would deliver her into *your* clutches. No! no! my scheming knaves, I will not. Kill me if you like, but it will not accomplish your villainous ends. She has all of the papers, and can not only put herself forward at the right time, but can have you arrested for my murder!"

"Bah! we can find her, as we have found you; so we will not trifle. Clarence, get ready; and when I count one—two—three—pull the trigger, and I'll finish him with my knife!"

"All right; go ahead; I'm ready!" replied the dutiful son.

Fearless Frank sat upon a bowlder in the mouth of the quartz mine, listening to the strains of music that floated up to him from the cabin out in the valley, and puffing moodily away at a grimy old pipe he had purchased, together with some tobacco, from one of the Utes, with whom he worked.

He had not gone down to the crusher-house for his supper; he did not feel hungry, and was more contented here, in the mouth of the mine, where he could command a view of all that was going on in the valley. With his pipe for a companion he was as happy as he could be, deprived as he was from association with the others of his color, who had barred him out in the cold.

Once or twice during the day, on coming from within, to get a breath of pure air, he had caught a glimpse of Anita as she flitted about the cabin engaged at her household duties, and the yearning expression that unconsciously stole into his dark eyes, spoke of a passion within his heart, that, though it might be slumbering, was not extinct—was there all the same, in all its strength and ardor. Had he been granted the privilege of meeting her, he might have displaced the barrier that rose between them; but now, nothing remained for him but to toil away until Redburn should see fit to send him away, back into the world from which he came.

Would he want to go, when that time came? Hardly, he thought, as he sat there and gazed into the quiet vale below him, so beautiful even in darkness. There was no reason why he should go back again adrift upon the bustling world.

He had no relatives—no claims that pointed him to go thither; he was as free and unfettered as the wildest mountain eagle. He had no one to say where he should and where he should not go; he liked one place equally as well as another, providing there was plenty of provender and work within easy range; he had never thought of settling down, until now, when he had come to the Flower Pocket valley, and caught a glimpse of Anita—Anita whom he had not seen for years; on whom he had brought censure, reproach and—

A step among the rocks close at hand startled him from a reverie into which he had fallen, and caused him to spill the tobacco from his pipe.

A slight trim figure stood a few yards away, and he perceived that two extended hands clasped objects, whose glistening surface suggested that they were "sixes" or "sevens."

"Silence!" came in a clear, authoritative voice. "One word more than I ask you, and I'll blow your brains out. Now, what's your name?"

"Justin McKenzie's my name. Fearless Frank generally answers me the purpose of a nom de plume," was the reply.

"Very good," and the stranger drew near enough for the Scarlet Boy to perceive that he was clad in buck-skin; well armed; wore a Spanish sombrero, and hair long, down over the square shoulders. "I'm Calamity Jane."

If McKenzie uttered an ejaculation of surprise, it was not to be wondered at, for he had heard many stories, in Deadwood, concerning the "dare-devil gal dressed up in men's toggery."

"Calamity Jane?" he echoed, picking up his pipe. "Where in the world did *you* come from, and how did you get here, and what do you want, and—"

"One at a time, please. I came from Deadwood with Road-Agent Dick's party—unknown to them, understand you. That answers two questions. The third is, I want to be around when there's any fun going on; and it's lucky I'm here now. I guess Dick has just got layed out by two fellows in the valley below here, and they've slid off with him over among the foot-hills yonder. I want you to stub along after me, and lend the voices of your sixes, if need be. I'm going to set him at liberty!"

"I'm at your service," Frank quickly replied. Excitement was one of his passions; adventure was another.

"Are you well heeled?"

"I reckon. Always make it a point to be prepared for wild beasts and the like, you know."

"A good idea. Well, if you are ready, we'll slide. I don't want them toughs to get the drop on Dick if I can help it."

"Who are they?"

"Who—the toughs?"

"Yes; they that took the road-agent"

"I don't know 'm. Guess they're tender-foots—some former enemies of his, without doubt. They propose to quiz a secret about some girl out of him, and then knife him. We'll have to hurry or they'll get their work in ahead of us."

They left the mouth of the mine, and skurried down into the valley, through the dense shroud of gloom.

Calamity Jane led the way; she was both fleet of foot and cautious.

Let us look down on the foot-hill camp, and the two Fillmores who are stationed on either side of their prisoner.

The younger presses the muzzle of his revolver against Deadwood Dick's heart; the elder holds a long gleaming knife upheld in his right hand.

"One!" he counts, savagely.

"Two!"—after a momentary pause. Another lapse of time, and then—

"Hold! gentlemen; that will do!" cries a clear ringing voice; and Calamity Jane and McKenzie, stepping out of the darkness, with four gleaming "sixes" in hand, confirm the pleasant assertion!

CHAPTER XVI.

THE ROAD-AGENT'S MERCY—CONCLUSION.

Nevertheless, the gleaming blade of Alexander Filmore descended, and was buried in the fleshy part of Deadwood Dick's neck, making a wound, painful but not necessarily dangerous.

"You vile varmint," cried Calamity Jane, pulling the hammer of one of her revolvers back to full cock; "you cursed fool; don't you know that that only seals yer own miserable fate?"

She took deliberate aim, but Dick interrupted her.

"Don't shoot, Jennie!" he gasped, the blood spurting from his wound; "this ain't none o' your funeral. Give three shrill whistles for my men, and they'll take care o' these hounds until I'm able to attend to 'em. Take me to the cab—"

He could not finish the sentence; a sickening stream of blood gushed from his mouth, and he fell back upon the ground insensible.

Fearless Frank gave the three shrill whistles, while Calamity Jane covered the two cowering wretches with her revolvers.

The distress signal was answered by a yell, and in a few seconds five road-agents came bounding up.

"Seize these two cusses, and guard 'em well!" Calamity said, grimly. "They are a precious pair, and in a few days, no doubt, you'll have the pleasure of attending their funerals. Your captain is wounded, but not dangerously, I hope. We will take him to the cabin, where there are light and skillful hands to dress his wounds. When he wants you, we will let you know. Be sure and guard these knaves well, now."

The men growled an assent, and after binding the captives' arms, hustled them off toward camp, in double quick time, muttering threats of vengeance. Fearless Frank and Calamity then carefully raised the stricken road-agent, and bore him to the cabin, where he was laid upon the couch. Of course, all was now excitement.

Redburn and Alice set to work to dress the bleeding wound, with Jane and the "General" looking on to see that nothing was left undone. Fearless Frank stood apart from the rest, his arms folded across his breast, a grave, half-doubtful expression upon his handsome, sun-browned features.

Anita was not in the room at the time, but she came in a moment later, and stood gazing about her in wondering surprise. Then, her eyes rested upon Fearless Frank for the first, and she grew deathly white; she trembled in every limb; a half-frightened, half-pitiful look came into her eyes.

The young man in scarlet was similarly effected. His cheeks blanched; his lips became firmly compressed; a mastering expression fell from his dark magnetic orbs.

There they stood, face to face, a picture of doubt; of indifferent respect, of opposite strong passions, subdued to control by a heavy hand.

None of the others noticed them; they were alone, confronting each other; trying to read the other's thoughts; the one penitent and craving forgiveness, the other cold almost to sternness, and yet not unwilling to forgive and forget.

Deadwood Dick's wound was quickly and skillfully dressed; it was not dangerous, but was so exceedingly painful that the pangs soon brought him back to consciousness.

The moment he opened his eyes he saw Fearless Frank and Anita—perceived their position toward each other, and that it would require only a single word to bridge the chasm between them. A hard look came into his eyes as they gazed through the holes in the mask, then he gazed at Alice—sweet piquant Alice—and the hardness melted like snow before the spring sunshine.

"Thank God it was no deeper," he said, sitting upright, and rubbing the tips of his black-glove fingers over the patches that covered the gash, "Although deucedly bothersome, it is not of much account."

To the surprise of all he sprung to his feet, and strode to the door. Here he stopped, and looked around for a few moments, sniffing at the cool mountain breeze, as a dog would. A single cedar tree stood by the cabin, its branches, bare and naked, stretching out like huge arms above the doorway. And it was at these the road-agent gazed, a savage gleam in his piercing black eyes.

After a few careful observations, he turned his face within the cabin.

"Justin McKenzie," he said, gazing at the young man, steadily, "I want you to do me a service. Go to my camp, and say to my men that I desire their presence here, together with the two prisoners, and a couple of stout lariats, with nooses at the end of them. Hurry, now!"

Fearless Frank started a trifle, for he seemed to recognize the voice; but the next instant he bowed assent, and left the cabin. When he was gone, Dick turned to Redburn.

"Have you a glass of water handy, Cap? This jab in the gullet makes me somewhat thirsty," he said.

Redburn nodded, and procured the drink; then a strange silence pervaded the cabin—a silence that no one seemed willing to break.

At last the tramp of many feet was heard, and a moment later the road-agents, with Fearless Frank at their head, reached the doorway, where they halted. The moment Deadwood Dick came forward, there was a wild, deafening cheer.

"Hurra! hurra! Deadwood Dick, Prince of the Road, still lives. Three long hearty cheers, lads, and a hummer!" cried Fearless Frank, and then the mountain echoes reverberated with a thousand discordant yells of hurrah.

The young road-agent responded with a nod, and then said:

"The prisoners; have you them there?"

"Here they are, Cap!" cried a score of voices, and the two Filmores were trotted out to the front, with ropes already about their necks. "Shall we h'ist 'em?"

"Not jest yet, boys: I have a few words to say, first."

Then turning half-about in the doorway, Deadwood Dick continued:

"Ladies and gentlemen, a little tragedy is about to take place here soon, and it becomes necessary that I should say a few words explaining what cause I have for hanging these two wretches whom you see here.

"Therefore, I will tell you a short story, and you will see that my cause is just, as we look at these things here in this delectable country of the Black Hills. To begin with:

"My name is, to you, *Edward Harris!*" and here the road-agent flung aside the black mask, revealing the smiling face of the young card-sharp. "I have another—my family name—but I do not use it, preferring Harris to it. Anita, yonder; is my sister.

"Several years ago, when we were children, living in one of the Eastern States, we were made orphans by the death of our parents, who were drowned while driving upon a frozen lake in company with my uncle, Alexander Filmore, and his son, Clarence—those are the parties yonder, and as God is my judge, I believe they are answerable for the death of our father and mother.

"Alexander Filmore was appointed guardian over us, and executor of our property, which amounted to somewhere in the neighborhood of fifty thousand dollars, my father having been for years extensively engaged in speculation, at which he was most always successful.

"From the day of their death we began to receive the most tyrannical treatment. We were whipped, kicked about, and kept in a half-starved condition. Twice when we were in bed, and, as he supposed, asleep, Alexander Filmore came to us and attempted to assassinate us, but my watchfulness was a match for his villainy, and we escaped death at his hands.

"Finding that this kind of life was unbearable, I appealed to our neighbors and even to the courts for protection, but my enemy was a man of great influence, and after many vain attempts, I found that I could not obtain a hearing; that nothing remained for me to do but to fight my own way. And I did fight it.

"Out of my father's safe I purloined a sum of money sufficient to defray our expenses for a while, and then, taking Anita with me, I fled from the home of my youth. I came first to Fort Laramie, where I spent a year in the service of a fur-trader.

"My guardian, during that year, sent three men out to kill me, but they had the tables turned on them, and their bones lay bleaching even now on Laramie plains.

"During that year my sister met a gay, dashing young ranger, who hailed to the name of Justin McKenzie, and of course she fell in love with him. That was natural, as he was handsome, suave and gallant, and, more than all, reported tolerably well to-do.

"I made inquiries, and found that there was nothing against his moral character, so I made no objections to his paying his attentions to Anita.

"But one day a great surprise came.

"On returning from a buffalo-hunt of several days' duration I found my home deserted, and a letter from Anita stating that she had gone with McKenzie to Cheyenne to live; they were not married yet, but would be, soon.

"That aroused the hellish part of my passionate nature. I believed that McKenzie was leading her a life of dishonor, and it made my blood boil to even think of it. Death, I swore, should be his reward for this infidelity, and mounting my horse I set out in hot haste for Cheyenne.

"But I arrived there too late to accomplish my mission of vengeance.

"I found Anita and took her back to my home, a sad and sorrowing maiden; McKenzie I could not find; he had heard of my coming, and fled to escape my avenging hand. But over the head of my weeping sister, I swore a fearful oath of vengeance, and I have it yet to keep. I believe there had been some kind of a sham marriage; Anita would never speak on the subject, so I had to guess at the terrible truth.

"And there's where you made an accursed mess of the whole affair!" cried McKenzie, stepping into the cabin, and leading Anita forward, by the hand. "Before-God and man *I acknowledge Anita Harris to be my legally wedded wife.* Listen, Edward Harris, and I will explain. That day that you came to Cheyenne in pursuit of me, I'll acknowledge I committed an error—one that has caused me much trouble since. The case was this:

"I was the nearest of kin to a rich old fur-trader, who proposed to leave me all his property at his death: but he was a desperate woman-hater, and bound me to a promise that I would never marry.

"Tempted by the lust for gold, I yielded, and he drew up a will in my favor. This was before I met Anita here.

"When we went to Cheyenne, the old man was lying at the point of death; so I told Anita that we would not be married for a few days, until we saw how matters were going to shape. If he died, we would be married secretly, and she would return to your roof until I could get possession of my inheritance, when we would go to some other part of the country to live. If he recovered, I would marry her anyway, and let the old man go to Tophet with his money-bags. I see now how I was in the wrong.

"Well, that very day, before your arrival, the old man himself pounced down upon us, and cursed me up hill and down, for my treachery, and forthwith struck me out from his will. I immediately sent for a chaplain, and was married to Anita. I then went up to see the old man and find if I could not effect a compromise with him.

"He told me if I would go with him before Anita and swear that she was not legally my wife, and that I would never live with her, he would again alter his will in my favor.

"Knowing that that would make no difference, so far as the law was concerned, I sent Anita a note apprising her of what was coming, and stating that she had best return to you until the old man should die, when I would come for her. Subsequently I went before her in company with the old man and swore as I had promised to do, and when I departed she was weeping bitterly, but I naturally supposed it was sham grief. A month later, on his death-bed, the old trader showed me the letter I had sent her, and I realized that not only was my little game up, but that I had cheated myself out of a love that was true. I was left entirely out of the will, and ever since I have bitterly cursed the day that tempted me to try to win gold and love at the same time. Here, Edward Harris," and the young man drew a packet of papers from inside his pocket, "are two certificates of my marriage, one for Anita, and one for myself. You see now, that, although mine has been a grievous error, no dishonor is coupled with your sister's name."

Ned Harris took one of the documents and glanced over it, the expression on his face softening. A moment later he turned and grasped McKenzie's hand.

"God bless you, old boy!" he said, huskily. "I am the one who has erred, and if you have it in your heart to forgive me, try and do so. I do not expect much quarter in this world, you know. There is Anita; take her, if she will come to you, and may God shower his eternal blessings upon you both!"

McKenzie turned around with open arms, and Anita flew to his embrace with a low glad cry. There was not a dry eye in the room.

There was an impatient surging of the crowd outside; Dick saw that his men were longing for the sport ahead; so he resumed his story:

"There is not much more to add," he said, after a moment's thought. "I fled into the Black Hills when the first whispers of gold got afloat, and chancing upon this valley, I built us a home here, wherein to live away the rest of our lives.

"In time I organized the band of men you see around me, and took to the road. Of this my sister knew nothing. The Hills have been my haunt ever since, and during all this time yon scheming knaves"— pointing to the prisoners—"have been constantly sending out men to murder me. The last tool, Hugh Vansevere by name, boldly posted up reward papers in the most frequented routes, and he went the same way as his predecessors. Seeing that nothing could be accomplished through aids, my enemies have at last come out to superintend my butchery in person; and but for the timely interference of Calamity Jane and Justin McKenzie, a short time since, I should have ere this been numbered with the dead. Now, I am inclined to be merciful to only those who have been merciful to me; therefore, I have decided that Alexander and Clarence Filmore shall pay the penalty of hanging, for their attempted crimes. Boys, *string 'em up!*"

So saying, Deadwood Dick stepped without the cabin, and closed the door behind him.

Redburn also shut down and curtained the windows, to keep out the horrible sight and sounds.

But, for all this, those inside could not help but hear the pleading cries of the doomed wretches, the tramp of heavy feet, the hushed babble of voices, and at last the terrible shout of, "Heave 'o! up they go!" which signaled the commencement of the victims' journey into mid-air.

Then there was a long blank pause; not a sound was heard, not a voice spoke, nor a foot moved. This silence was speedily broken, however, by two heavy falls, followed almost immediately by the tramp of feet.

Not till all was again quiet did Redburn venture to open the door and look out. All was dark and still.

The road-agents had gone, and left no sign of their work behind.

When morning dawned, they were seen to have re-camped on the eastern slope, where the smoke of their camp-fires rose in graceful white columns through the clear transparent atmosphere.

During the day Dick met Alice Terry, as she was gathering flowers, a short distance from the cabin.

"Alice—Miss Terry," he said, gravely, "I have come to ask you to be my wife. I love you, and want you for my own darling. Be mine, Alice, and I will mend my ways, and settle down to an honest, straightforward life."

The beautiful girl looked up pityingly.

"No," she said, shaking her head, her tone kind and respectful, "I cannot love you, and never can be your wife, Mr. Harris."

"You love another?" he interrogated.

She did not answer, but the tell-tale blush that suffused her cheek did, for her.

"It is Redburn!" he said, positively. "Very well; give him my congratulations. See, Alice;" here the young road-agent took the crape mask from his bosom; "I now resume the wearing of this mask. Your refusal has decided my future. A merry road-agent I have been, and a merry road-agent I shall die. Now, good-by forever."

On the following morning it was discovered that the road-agents and their daring leader, together with the no less heroic Calamity Jane, had left the valley—gone; whither, no one knew.

About a month later, one day when Calamity Jane was watering her horse at the stream, two miles above Deadwood, the road-agent chief rode out of the chaparral and joined her.

He was still masked, well armed, and looking every inch a Prince of the Road.

"Jennie," he said, reining in his steed, "I am lonely and want a companion to keep me company through life. You have no one but yourself; our spirits and general temperament agree. Will you marry me and become my queen?"

"No!" said the girl, haughtily, sternly. "I have had all the *man* I care for. We can be friends, Dick; more we can never be!"

"Very well, Jennie; I rec'on it is destined that I shall live single. At any rate, I'll never take a refusal from another woman. Yes, gal, we'll be friends, if nothing more."

There is little more to add.

We might write at length, but choose a few words to end this o'er true romance of life in the Black Hills.

McKenzie and Anita were remarried in Deadwood, and at the same time Redburn led Alice Terry to the altar, which consummation the "General" avowed was "more or less of a good thing—consider'bly less o' more 'n' more o' less."

Through eastern lawyers, a settlement of the Harris affairs was effected, the whole of the property being turned over to Anita, thereby placing her and Fearless Frank above want for a lifetime.

Therefore they gave up their interest in the Flower Pocket mines to Redburn and the "General."

Calamity Jane is still in the Hills.

And grim and uncommunicative, there roams through the country of gold a youth in black, at the head of a bold lawless gang of road-riders, who, from his unequaled daring, has won and rightly deserves the name—Deadwood Dick, Prince of the Road.

THE END.

Edward L. Wheeler's

Deadwood Dick Novels

IN

Beadle's Half-Dime Library.

- 1. Deadwood Dick; or, The Black Rider of the Black Hills.
- 20. The Double Daggers; or, Deadwood Dick's Defiance.
- 28. Buffalo Ben; or, Deadwood Dick in Disguise.
- 35. Wild Ivan, the Boy Claude Duval; or, The Brotherhood of Death.
- 42. The Phantom Miner; or, Deadwood Dick's Bonanza.
- 49. Omaha Oll; or, Deadwood Dick in Danger.
- 75. Deadwood Dick's Eagles; or, The Pards of Flood Bar.
- 73. Deadwood Dick on Deck; or, Calamity Jane, the Heroine of Whoop-Up.
- 77. Corduroy Charlie; or, The Last Act of Deadwood Dick.
- 100. Deadwood Dick in Leadville; or, A Strange Stroke for Liberty.
- 104. Deadwood Dick's Device; or, The Sign of the Double Cross.
- 109. Deadwood Dick as Detective.
- 121. Cinnamon Chip, the Girl Sport; or, The Golden Idol of Mount Rosa.
- 129. Deadwood Dick's Double; or, The Ghost of Gordon's Gulch.
- 138. Blonde Bill; or, Deadwood Dick's Home Base.
- 149. A Game of Gold; or, Deadwood Dick's Big Strike.
- 156. Deadwood Dick of Deadwood; or, The Picked Party.
- 195. Deadwood Dick's Dream; or, The Rivals of the Road.
- 201. The Black Hills Jezebel; or, Deadwood Dick's Ward.
- 205. Deadwood Dick's Doom; or, Calamity-Jane's Last Adventure.
- 217. Captain Crack-Shot, the Girl Brigand; or, Gypsy Jack from Jimtown.

- 221. Sugar Coated Sam; or, The Black Gowns of Grim Gulch.

The above are for sale by all newsdealers, five cents a copy, or sent by mail on receipt of six cents each.

CPSIA information can be obtained at www.ICGtesting.com
Printed in the USA
LVOW051509120812

293927LV00003B/108/P